D0938824

MURDER
IN THE
BALL PARK

Center Point
Large Print

Also by Robert Goldsborough and available from Center Point Large Print:

The Nero Wolfe Mysteries
Archie Meets Nero Wolfe

**This Large Print Book carries the
Seal of Approval of N.A.V.H.**

MURDER
IN THE
BALL PARK

A Nero Wolfe Mystery

Robert Goldsborough

CENTER POINT LARGE PRINT
THORNDIKE, MAINE

This Center Point Large Print edition
is published in the year 2014 by arrangement with
The Mysterious Press.

The text of this Large Print edition is unabridged.
In other aspects, this book may vary
from the original edition.
Printed in the United States of America
on permanent paper.
Set in 16-point Times New Roman type.

ISBN: 978-1-62899-147-5

Library of Congress Cataloging-in-Publication Data

Goldsborough, Robert.
 Murder in the ball park : a Nero Wolfe mystery / Robert Goldsborough.
 — Center Point Large Print edition.
 pages ; cm.
 Summary: "When a sniper kills a senator at a ballgame, Nero Wolfe is
called upon to solve the murder"—Provided by publisher.
 ISBN 978-1-62899-147-5 (library binding : alk. paper)
 1. Wolfe, Nero (Fictitious character)—Fiction.
    2. Private investigators—New York (State)—New York—Fiction.
    3. Murder—Fiction. 4. Large type books. I. Title.
 PS3557.O3849M84 2014
 813'.54—dc23
                                                    2014012969

To Max Allan Collins,
a superb writer,
a loyal friend and confidant,
and a generous encourager

MURDER
IN THE
BALL PARK

CHAPTER 1

Saul Panzer and I have been going to baseball games in New York for years, almost since I started working for Nero Wolfe. Somehow, I became a Giants fan early on, probably because a satisfied client of Wolfe's gave me tickets to a game at the Polo Grounds the first year that I lived and toiled in the old brownstone on West Thirty-Fifth Street over near the Hudson River.

For those of you new to these narratives, some words about Saul Panzer before we move on. Truth be told, he will not bowl you over with his appearance. He stands about five foot seven, and I doubt he'd push the needle on a bathroom scale beyond the 140 mark. His wrinkled mug is about two-thirds nose, and he invariably needs a shave. He has rust-colored hair that rarely sees a comb, and his shoulders stoop, one lower than the other. He's usually garbed in an old suit, gray or brown, and a battered flat cap that's every bit as old as his suits.

But do not for a single moment let the man's appearance fool you. Saul happens to be the best freelance operative—by far—in what is this country's largest city—by far. He makes himself invisible when he's holding a tail, and he sniffs out clues better than the finest bloodhound pacing nervously in the police kennel. Because of this, and other attributes, he always has more business than he can handle, although he has been known to drop any case he's working on to tackle a job for Nero Wolfe when asked.

He admires Wolfe, and the feeling is reciprocated. "I trust Saul more than might be thought credible," Wolfe has said on several occasions—a feeling I strongly second. A bachelor, Saul lives on the top floor of a remodeled building on East Thirty-Eighth Street. His digs include a spacious living room with floor-to-ceiling bookcases filled with—yes—books, several museum-quality oil paintings on the walls, a grand piano, and a bar well stocked with brands that boast quality labels.

The best poker player I have had the bad fortune to go up against, Saul makes good money—both with cards and as a detective—and he invests it wisely. He owns two buildings in Brooklyn that I'm aware of and currently has his eye on another one.

While we're on the subject of Brooklyn, Saul is a lifelong Dodgers fan, which is how we happen to attend two games a season together—one each at the Polo Grounds and at Ebbets Field over on the other side of the East River in Brooklyn. This tradition began when Saul ragged me about rooting for the Giants. The result was that we bet on each of the games we attend, with the loser buying dinner at Rusterman's Restaurant in Midtown Manhattan, the world-class eatery owned and operated by Marko Vukčić, Nero Wolfe's oldest and best friend.

We've been fairly even in the years since we began this ongoing wager, although I had won the last two times and was feeling pretty confident that sunny mid-June afternoon in the Polo Grounds up at the north end of Manhattan, given that the Giants were leading the league and were several games ahead of the Dodgers, the preseason league favorites, who were struggling in third place.

"Archie, old friend, I can sense your smugness," Saul said with a sly grin as we slid into our front-row seats slightly to the third-base side of home plate and halfway between the two dugouts. He was barely seated when he fired up one of those foul-smelling Egyptian cigarettes he insists on buying. "But pride cometh before a fall, and my beloved Bums have their best pitcher going today, none other than Ace Farley. I see a free meal at Rusterman's in my very near future. I can almost taste the *tournedos Beauharnais* that you will be treating me to, Mr. Goodwin."

"Not so fast, transplanted Brooklynite. You know that we've got our own top hurler going, Hawk Harrigan, who's won his last six games, three of them shutouts. So I fully expect that this very evening, I will be feasting on *perdrix en casserole*, courtesy of one S. Panzer, misguided Dodgers aficionado. As for the *tournedos*, feel free to order them. After all, you're the one who will be picking up the tab."

The raillery over, we settled back in our seats, each with a beer and a hot dog, and awaited the start of the game. We quickly got to our feet, however, as "The Star-Spangled Banner" blared in a static-filled recording as a group of some twenty Boy Scouts in uniform trooped smartly onto the field, each of them holding an American flag high.

When the national anthem ended, the public address announcer informed us that today was Flag Day, and that the Giants were honoring the Stars and Stripes. As the Scouts marched off the field, an entourage led by a uniformed usher made its way down the aisle to our right. The procession of five, all of them smiling and waving small American flags, was led by a lean, white-haired man with chiseled features and a three-piece plaid suit that looked like it would cost your average working stiff six months' wages.

"You know just about everybody important in this town. Who's the swell with the snow on his summit?" I asked Saul, gesturing toward the fashion plate.

"Archie, that 'swell,' as you choose to term him, is none other than the Honorable Orson David

Milbank, a state senator representing some of the most well-heeled residents of the Empire State—the three counties just north of the city and east of the mighty Hudson. And he is pretty well heeled himself. His father made a fortune in the scrap-metal business, and Orson inherited most of it. He'll never have to work another day in his life, unless you count sitting in the capitol up in Albany deciding how to spend the state's money. Or more properly, *our* money."

"Milbank—oh yeah, he's been in the news a lot lately, right? The one who's trying to block a new road being planned to run north from the city?"

"That's your man. Lots of residents in his district up the Hudson are dead-set against this Northern Parkway, as they're calling it. Those folks moved up there to get away from the hectic pace of the metropolis, and they see the road as an infringement upon their God-given, bucolic, country-squire way of life. A lot of them may work in New York City, but they don't like the idea of living here, heaven forbid," Saul said with a scowl.

"So who's in favor of the road?"

"A lot of businesses, the local chambers of commerce, and real estate agents and developers, as you would expect. They all view it as a potential boon to the local economy."

"What are the odds of the thing being built?"

Saul shrugged. "I haven't followed the maneuverings all that closely, but I can tell you this much: Milbank is taking a lot of heat from commercial interests up north who want to see the road built. It seems the senator has got some skeletons they threaten to haul out of his closet."

"Like what?"

"Just for starters, some of those millionaire gentlemen farmers in his district are said to have been slipping him money, big money, under the table to block the parkway—as if he needs more dough. And one of those so-called farmers happens to be Franco Bacelli."

"Meaning, of course, the senator is in bed with the Mob and its kingpin. You said that's just for starters?"

Saul nodded. "Our Mr. Milbank has been in bed with more than the Mob, or so his detractors claim."

"As in his love life?"

"Archie, as I have so often said, you are one quick study. The senator is on his second wife, the much-younger Elise DuVal, a flashy redhead who acted—if you can call it that—in a couple of grade-B Hollywood films a few years back. She also happens to be on marriage number two herself. Word is that neither of them pays much attention to their wedding vows."

"Come to think of it, I've seen that lovely lady's picture in the paper on occasion. Having been divorced doesn't seem to have stopped the man from being elected," I observed.

"And reelected, a number of times," Saul said. "His first wife apparently had some serious mental problems and is in an institution, so the public has generally sympathized with him."

"You are a veritable font of information," I told Saul. "Where do you amass all of this knowledge?"

"On slow days, I admit to reading the gossip columns in the tabloids," he said between sips of beer. "For instance, I know from these columns that the nicely constructed blonde wearing blue and sitting just to the right of the senator is his press secretary, one Mona Fentress, and that she and Milbank spend a lot of time together, planning . . . well, strategy."

"Pardon my political ignorance," I said, "but why does a mere state senator even need a press secretary?"

"Most of them don't need one, or have one, but Orson Milbank thinks big. He has dreams that stretch far beyond the confines of Albany, so I've read," Saul answered. "The political columns say he's got his eye on getting a seat in that *real* senate, the one that meets in Washington, so it helps to have someone who can get your name in the papers, and frequently. But that's enough talk of this puffed-up politician. Let's watch some baseball."

That's what we did, and good baseball it was—if, like me, you enjoy good pitching. For three-plus innings, Harrigan and Farley showed why they were the top men on their respective pitching staffs, mowing down the opponents' batters with surgical efficiency. Each team had only one hit going into the New York fourth, when Reed Mason, the Giants' best hitter, smashed a line drive to left field. The small weekday gathering of a few thousand rose with a cheer as the ball barely cleared the close-in wall less than three hundred feet from home plate and just beyond the reach of the Dodgers' leaping left fielder.

I was among those cheering, and as I turned to slap Saul on the back, I saw that the Milbank entourage had turned inward, all of them looking down rather than admiring the path of the home run. I realized the tableau lacked one figure—the white-haired senator himself.

"Oh my God, help! Someone please help!" Mona Fentress keened, hands pressed to cheeks as she sunk to her knees. "The senator, the senator . . ."

I don't remember now, but I may very well have knocked someone down as I ran to the huddled cluster of people in the senator's box. Milbank, arms akimbo, was draped across his seat and the armrest of the one next to him, ice-blue eyes staring skyward and mouth open.

"Shot," Saul snapped from behind me, pointing

to a crimson hole in the left side of Milbank's head.

"Is he . . . ?" one of the senator's lackeys asked.

Panzer nodded after pressing his fingers against Milbank's carotid. "Shot, but from where?" he asked. All of us looked toward the yawning grandstands in left field, which were empty as is often the case on weekday afternoon games.

By now, ushers and a lone uniformed policeman had converged on the scene as a collective gasp came from the crowd. Both dugouts emptied, with the Giants and Dodgers changing roles from performers to awed spectators as they stared toward the seats in the first row.

The cop, a thickset, red-faced sergeant named Blake, elbowed his way past all of us and stared down at Milbank. "All right, everybody clear the area now—out, all of you. This is a crime scene, and the medics are on the way. Let's give them some room now, everybody."

"Sounds like a good idea," I told Saul. "I don't want to be here when Inspector Cramer or, heaven forbid, his dull-witted, stuttering underling, Lieutenant George Rowcliff, shows up. Each of them would try to pin this on me somehow."

"Archie, I'm with you all the way. I have a feeling there will be no more baseball today, and there's nothing we can contribute by hanging around here. How 'bout we each pick up our own check at Rusterman's tonight?"

"A capital idea indeed," I said. "We just witnessed what, of course, was a murder, and for once, I won't be trying to talk Wolfe into taking the case." At the time I spoke those words, I really meant them.

CHAPTER 2

For the next week and then some, the city's intensely competitive daily newspapers vented about Senator Orson Milbank's very public shooting, which was widely accepted as premeditated murder.

"When an esteemed and respected public figure is assassinated in a public arena, surrounded by thousands of his fellow citizens, rampant and unbridled lawlessness has truly permeated our city," the *New York Daily Mirror* raged in a front-page editorial under the headline THE WILD WEST COMES TO MANHATTAN. Its rival tabloid, the *New York Daily News*, offered a fifty-thousand-dollar reward for information leading to the capture of the gunman, whom the police believe fired from the upper deck of the Polo Grounds' left-field stands. The *Gazette* weighed in with its own editorial that called the killing "an affront to each and every law-abiding citizen of this city and this state." The *New York Times* editorial termed the event "yet another example of a societal breakdown in the nation's fabric."

The mayor felt the heat, as did Police Commissioner Humbert, who in a press conference boasted, "The department is marshaling all of its considerable resources in the hunt for this vicious and brazen killer, and we shall not stop until he is apprehended and brought to the justice that he so rightly deserves."

After the commissioner had finished his scripted statement, the reporters climbed all over him, demanding to know what progress had been made. "I have no further comment at this time," Humbert harrumphed, storming from the lectern and retreating to the sanctuary of his office.

From the beginning, Nero Wolfe viewed the Milbank affair with a marked lack of interest. After all, he currently enjoyed an unusually healthy bank balance, having just successfully wrapped up a lucrative case in which a wealthy Connecticut dowager's Cézanne landscape painting got safely returned to her. The valuable oil had disappeared from her Fairfield County mansion, and Wolfe, without leaving his sturdy office chair—but with my invaluable observations from sniffing around the lady's sprawling estate—had identified the thief, one of the estate's groundskeepers, who now awaited trial in our neighboring state to the east.

On a sunny morning, I sat at my desk in the office, typing the letters Wolfe had dictated the previous afternoon, when the phone rang. "Nero Wolfe's office, Archie Goodwin speaking," I pronounced into the mouthpiece.

"Hello, Mr. Archie Goodwin, I would like to

make an appointment with Nero Wolfe." The voice was female, soft, and silky. I liked it.

"May I ask the reason for your appointment?"

"You may. My name is Elise DuVal. It is possible that you have heard of me."

"It is possible," I agreed.

"Are you toying with me, Archie Goodwin?"

"By no means, Miss DuVal! Let it never be said that I treat a potential client with anything less than the fullest respect. Nonetheless, I will repeat my question: What is the reason for your wanting to see Nero Wolfe?"

"As I am led to believe, you, like Mr. Wolfe, are a licensed private investigator. As such, you need not even have to ask that question. I assume you read the newspapers and listen to the radio and now even watch the television, so the answer should be obvious to you."

"Perhaps I am somewhat dense, as has been suggested by a number of people. I would like to hear the answer from your very own lips."

Elise DuVal's exaggerated sigh came through the wire. "All right, here it is, as if you didn't already know: I want Nero Wolfe—which I suppose means you, as well—to find my husband's killer."

"But isn't that precisely what the police are attempting to do—and around the clock, no less?"

"Hah! Attempting is the word. It has been ten days now, if you have been counting, and they are absolutely nowhere. I have been to see that idiot

Commissioner Humbert, and also to see Inspector Cramer. He—Cramer, I mean—is no idiot, but he seems to be every bit as lost as Humbert. From everything I've been hearing, when your boss accepts a case, he always gets results."

"You are correct, but first he has to agree to take a case, and often—very often—that is the hardest part."

"He will accept the case if I can see him, and I gather that is where you come in. I understand from my very well-placed sources that you are the gatekeeper, right?"

"I guess you could say so, among my many other functions here. But before I can try to persuade Mr. Wolfe, you need to persuade me that it's worth my time to argue with him."

"It seems to me that he would relish the challenge," Elise said. "A high-profile story like this. Just think of the publicity he would get."

"Miss DuVal, you may possess what you believe are well-placed sources, but it is clear you don't know as much about Nero Wolfe as you think. Over the years, he has amassed mountains of attention—we have scrapbooks filled with newspaper clippings to attest to his success. At this stage, he does not feel he needs more publicity, nor does he go out of his way to seek it."

"But he surely doesn't say no to more money, does he?" she purred. "And believe me, money is not an issue here. I am prepared to bring a blank check to you and have Mr. Wolfe fill in an amount."

Now Elise DuVal really did have my full attention. "Before we go on, do you have any theories as to who shot your husband?"

"It could be any one of several people. As you probably are aware, Orson had made more than a few enemies during his years up in Albany. He was a man of strong personal convictions."

"I assume you have given the names of these enemies to the police."

She sniffed. "Of course I have. But the department did not seem to take me seriously."

"That does not sound like the Inspector Cramer I have come to know. He takes everything seriously, particularly murder."

"Oh, he did jot down some notes, of course, and he asked me a few questions. But I got the distinct impression that he felt I was wasting his time."

"Where were you when the shooting took place, Miss DuVal?"

"Up in Albany. We rent an apartment there, given that Orson spends—spent—so much of his time in that burg. Between us, I don't particularly like Albany, but I was there because Orson had a fund-raising dinner scheduled at one of their downtown hotels the next night, and he had asked me to be on the dais with him. I went up a day early on an afternoon train, about the same time as . . . as that baseball game."

23

"Other than the Albany apartment, where is home?"

Orson's legal address was his late parents' home in Pawling. That allowed him to fulfill the residency requirement for holding office.

"We have a duplex just off Park Avenue. In fact, one of our neighbors is a good friend of yours—in fact, a *very* good friend."

I knew where she was going, but I was damned if I was going to give her any help. "Is that so?" I said. "It may surprise you to learn that I happen to have a lot of good friends."

"I said a *very* good friend. And you know precisely who I am talking about—Lily Rowan."

"Ah, of course. And how is Lily?"

"I am surprised that you would ask, Mr. Goodwin. I telephoned her first thing this morning before calling you, and she said the two of you spent last night dancing at the Flamingo Club until late into the evening. She informs me you are a superb dancer."

"Modesty forbids me from responding."

"I am sure that it does. Now what about my appointment with Nero Wolfe?" Her tone had hardened ever so slightly.

"I will speak to him about it this very day."

"When he comes down from the plant rooms?" she asked. "I know he is up there with his orchids and his gardener, Theodore Horstmann, every day from nine to eleven in the morning and four

24

to six in the afternoon, almost without exception."

"You seem to know a great deal about Mr. Wolfe's routine."

"Lily has filled me in on all sorts of things, from those orchids to the wonderful meals you enjoy on a daily basis, cooked by a man named Fritz Brenner. She tells me he works wonders in the kitchen."

I made a mental note to ask Lily about her persistent neighbor and told Elise DuVal I would get back to her. When she pressed me as to exactly when she would be hearing from me, I ended the conversation with "I've got to go now; Mr. Wolfe is on his way down from those plant rooms you mentioned."

Which happened to be true. At two minutes after eleven by my watch, Nero Wolfe strode into the office and placed a raceme of purple-maroon cymbidium in the vase on his desk. "Good morning, Archie, did you sleep well?" he asked as he moved behind his desk and settled into the custom-built chair designed to accommodate his seventh of a ton.

"Like a baby who just won the Irish Sweep-stakes," I said.

He ignored my remark and began signing the letters I had typed and placed on his blotter. When he finished, I swiveled to face him. "We have a potential client who wants to see you," I said.

"I am otherwise occupied," he snapped,

25

reaching for the button under his desk drawer to ring Fritz in the kitchen for beer.

"Really? Occupied with what? You have just signed all of your correspondence, which I will mail. You have no appointments this week or next, according to the calendar I so faithfully keep for you, unless you count your twice-daily trips up to the plant rooms to play with your orchids. I realize the bank balance is healthy at the moment, but you know how fast that can evaporate, what with the pending arrival of the gas bill, the electric bill, the phone bill, the grocery bill, and the beer bill. Then, of course, you've got my salary to worry about, plus those of Fritz, without whom you would starve, and Theodore, without whom your orchids would starve. And then there's—"

"Archie, you are prattling!"

"Yes, sir, it is a bad habit of mine, as you know. It's just that this potential client is prepared to hand you a blank check and have you ink in the amount."

"Is this twaddle?" Wolfe glared at me as Fritz entered from the kitchen with two chilled bottles of beer and a glass on a tray.

"No, sir, it is not. The person wanting to see you is Elise DuVal, who is—"

"I know who she is. I read the newspapers. Preposterous."

"And just what is so preposterous about a blank

check that is just waiting for you to fill in the figure of your liking?"

"My adjective refers to the reason the woman surely wants to hire me," Wolfe said, draining half the beer from his glass and dabbing his lips with a handkerchief. "At this very moment, countless members of New York's police force are assigned to finding the individual who shot that senator."

"I pointed that out to her, of course, but Elise DuVal feels that out city's finest are not doing a good job."

"Nonetheless, Inspector Cramer is a general with an army under his command. As you know, the most I could marshal are three or four men, albeit able ones."

"There is one more thing I should mention."

"Yes?"

"Miss DuVal is a very good friend of Miss Rowan." I concede the "very good" was an overstatement.

That earned me a glower. Ever since the first time Lily asked to see his ten thousand orchids in the three climate-controlled plant rooms on the roof, Wolfe has exempted her from his usual antipathy toward women. In fact, on those occasions when she drops by the brownstone, he seems almost pleased to see her, although I would never let on to him that I notice.

"How do the women happen to know each

other?" Wolfe asked. I explained that they are neighbors, and he leaned back, closing his eyes and interlacing his hands over his middle mound. After several minutes, he opened his eyes and sighed. "Tell Miss DuVal to be here tomorrow morning at eleven."

CHAPTER 3

That afternoon when Wolfe was back up in the plant rooms, I telephoned Elise DuVal and told her he would see her.

"That's wonderful news! Tell me what I can do to get him to take me on as a client, Archie."

Obviously, she now felt we were on a first-name basis. "For starters, do not try to get cute with Mr. Wolfe, whatever else you do," I said. "Just because he has agreed to see you does not mean he will go to work for you. If I were taking book, I'd call it a long shot, three-to-one against. Be straightforward and businesslike when you come here."

"Archie, I am always straightforward and strictly business. Cross my heart."

"I'll take your word for that. One more thing: Be prompt. When Mr. Wolfe says eleven o'clock, that is what he means—not five after."

"I will be on time, I promise. What should I wear?"

"I am hardly qualified to act as a fashion consultant. Because you are coming here to discuss business, the best I can do is to suggest you dress in a businesslike manner. Which I am sure you will."

"I will be the very picture of decorum, Archie."

My next call was to Lily Rowan. "Escamillo," she purred, using a pet name she had tagged me with several years earlier after I had a run-in with a charging bull in an upstate meadow, "am I to assume you are perhaps phoning to pump me for information about a certain fetching neighbor of mine who once was employed as an actress in that debauched California town?"

"By chance, would you be referring to Hollywood?"

"I would."

"Then you assume right. Elise DuVal, or the recently widowed Mrs. Orson Milbank if you prefer, has an appointment to see Mr. Wolfe tomorrow morning."

"Ah, so he is going to take on the case," Lily said. "Interesting news. When she asked me about him, I said he probably wouldn't have anything to do with it. I must say that I am surprised."

"Hold your surprise. He's only agreed to see her, and I suspect that is mainly because she claims to be a friend of yours."

"I am flattered," Lily said, "although I wouldn't strictly term Elise a friend. Oh, she is a resident of this building, and with a very pleasing and well-decorated duplex, and she's a decent sort, if you can get past those affectations that probably result from having spent too much time with those motion-picture types. We've attended several of the same parties over the last few years and we both serve on a couple of charitable committees—'do-gooder groups' as you persist in calling them. But other than that, we tend to travel in different social circles."

"You have never introduced me to her, and I've never even heard you mention her," I said, trying to sound hurt.

"I was merely trying to protect you, my dear. I feared that you might fall victim to her considerable charms."

"Indeed a risk," I conceded. "What else can you tell me about the lady?"

"I have always felt her marriage to the late senator was one of convenience—for them both," Lily pronounced. "I'm sure she looked splendid on his arm at state dinners and other formal functions. And he helped fulfill her need to be in a limelight of sorts, now that her acting career appears to be history."

"Speaking of that career, I haven't seen her on the silver screen, but I gather that La DuVal was never a candidate to win an Academy Award."

Lily laughed. "Any response I give to that is going to make me seem catty, Escamillo."

"I hereby attest that whatever you say will remain strictly between us," I told her. "I have never called you catty, and I never will."

"That is only because you are such a gentleman. Okay, here goes. Several years ago, before I knew Elise, I did see one of the films she was in, and it was obvious to me that she had been cast for her, well . . . physical attributes, rather than any real or perceived acting abilities. Funny thing, though: As I have gotten to know her, I've come to realize that she's a very bright, personable individual, quite likable. I think those Hollywood types purposely cast her as a 'Dumb Dora' and gave her inane lines. So maybe there was really a decent actress trying to break out from under all of that ridiculous and stupid dialogue that she got stuck parroting."

"Could be. You said theirs was a marriage of convenience. I've heard talk—and that's all it is —that both she and her late husband may not have strictly honored their wedding vows."

"And I have heard the same thing, more than once," Lily answered. "I don't have specific knowledge of any hanky-panky, although it would not surprise me on the part of either one of them."

"A wonderful phrase, 'hanky-panky.' I must try to work it into a conversation sometime."

"Just don't work it into your repertoire," Lily said archly.

"To think that you would suspect me of such knavery. Anything else you feel I should know about the former Hollywood starlet?"

"I don't think so, except to say that whatever her relationship was with the late senator, I can tell you based on what I've heard from mutual acquaintances that she is genuinely broken up over what has happened. On that front, she definitely is not acting."

At five minutes before eleven the next morning, our bell rang, and by prearrangement with Fritz, I did the honors, pulling open the front door to reveal one of the finest specimens of womanhood ever to call upon us. Elise DuVal may not have been a fine actress, but she certainly knew how to accent her more obvious assets, from her wavy red hair down to her well-shaped ankles. To her credit, she had chosen to wear a subdued green suit that qualified as businesslike, although it failed to camouflage her most prominent assets.

"Hello, Mr. Archie Goodwin," she chirped with a tilt of the head and the raising of an eyebrow. "I must say, Lily described you very well. If you are through devouring me with your eyes, will you invite me inside? I certainly do not want to be accused of keeping Nero Wolfe waiting."

I stepped aside to let her in, admiring the way she moved, self-assured but not arrogant, displaying her charms but not flaunting them. I seated her in the red leather chair, aware the positioning would afford Wolfe a good view of her legs—legs that were worth viewing.

Elise had just settled into the chair when Wolfe entered, moving behind his desk, placing lavender orchids in his vase, and dipping his chin toward her. "Miss DuVal," he said, sitting.

"Mr. Wolfe," she responded with a slight smile and a nod, making no attempt to hold out a paw to him. Lily Rowan had likely briefed her about Wolfe's aversion to shaking hands.

"Would you like something to drink?" he asked. "I am having beer."

"No, thank you, nothing," she said demurely, gloved hands in her lap.

"Very well," he said after he had opened his first beer and poured it. "Mr. Goodwin tells me you wish to hire me. Am I correct in assuming it is to identify the individual who killed your husband?"

"Of course, you are correct!" she said, crossing one nylon-sheathed leg over the other and leaning forward. "As I told Arch—Mr. Goodwin, the police have gotten nowhere in their so-called investigation."

He drank beer and raised his eyebrows. "What makes you think I can improve upon their performance?"

I waited with interest for Elise's response, aware of how much Wolfe dislikes flattery.

She cleared her throat. "You know a neighbor of mine, Lily Rowan. She has told me about some of the cases you have solved—cases that had totally stymied the New York Police Department. Now the police are yet again stymied. I have full confidence that you can identify my husband's killer."

Wolfe scowled. "That is more confidence than I possess, madam. Also, at present I am not accepting commissions. I agreed to see you only because you are an acquaintance of Miss Rowan, who has been a guest in this house on numerous occasions."

Elise nodded, shifted in her chair, and drew a blank check from her purse, placing it on a corner of Wolfe's desk with a flourish worthy of an on-screen gesture. She produced a gold fountain pen and began to write. I swiveled from my desk and by craning my neck was able to see the figure she put down. This was no longer a blank check. In fact, if it was not the largest retainer ever offered to Nero Wolfe, it easily ranked among the top ten.

"Will this persuade you to make an exception?" she asked, sliding the check toward Wolfe with a manicured finger.

He eyed the draft without expression, considering Elise with narrowed eyes. "Madam, I would be guilty of dissembling if I were to say your offer did not tempt me," he said. "Any man who proclaims that he cannot be purchased is either a liar or a lackwit, or perhaps both."

"So you accept?" Elise asked, squaring her shoulders and breaking into a grin that belonged in a magazine advertisement for toothpaste.

"I do not, madam," Wolfe said, pushing the

check back toward her with an index finger. "I am tempted, to be sure, but am not now prepared to make a commitment. I must excuse myself, but I suggest you remain and discuss with Mr. Goodwin your suspicions as to who you feel killed your husband, and why. You will find him to be a thorough investigator. After your conversation, he will report to me and I will consider your request."

He stood, dipped his chin again, and walked out of the office. His destination surely was the kitchen, where he would attempt to supervise Fritz's preparation of the broiled shad with sorrel sauce we would have for lunch.

CHAPTER 4

I knew what Wolfe was up to, of course, just as he knew that I knew. If he had turned Elise DuVal down flat, I would have badgered him endlessly about the big payday he was passing up. This way, he threw the ball to me and delayed his decision, as well as freeing himself from spending more time in the presence of a woman, albeit an attractive one. When asked, Wolfe will insist that he does not dislike the female sex. "They are astonishing and successful animals," he once told me, adding that "for reasons of convenience, I merely preserve an appearance of immunity that I developed some years ago under the pressure of necessity." When I pressed him further, he changed the subject, and over the years has consistently avoided being around women more than absolutely necessary, with the occasional exception of Lily.

After Wolfe's exit, Elise turned to me and cocked her head. "Well, Archie Goodwin, does this mean that you are going to give me the third degree?"

"The police give criminal suspects the third degree," I replied, "but private investigators ask deep and probing questions of clients."

"Well, probe away, sir," she said as I moved to

one of the yellow chairs and faced her, our knees almost touching.

"Okay, for starters, do you have any prime suspects?"

"You go right to the point, don't you, Archie?"

"I don't believe in wasting anyone's time, ours or that of a potential client," I said, grinning.

She made a face. "So I am still only a *potential* client?"

"For the moment, you are. Of course, it is possible that may change."

"Our conversation is confidential, isn't it?" she asked. "I would not want to be sued for libel."

"If there were a charge, it would be for slander, not libel. And this is a fine time to be asking such a question. It should go without saying that everything discussed here is confidential. And, after all, you told us you have already given names to the police. Do you trust them more than you trust Mr. Wolfe and me?"

"No, of course, I don't. You are absolutely right. All right, here goes, and—wait, I see that you don't have something to write on, Archie."

"I almost never take notes. Believe me, it's all kept up here," I told her, tapping my forehead with a finger.

"Mark me down as being impressed."

"As you should be. Okay, it's time to talk suspects. Fire away."

Elise crossed her legs, her dark blue eyes locked

on to me as if daring me to look down at those shapely gams. I resisted the impulse, grinning and holding her gaze. "You were about to say?"

"Where to start?" she said, exhaling. "Does the name Jonah Keller mean anything to you?"

"A big-shot real estate operator up north of here, isn't he?"

"That is putting it mildly, Archie," she sniffed with a toss of her head. "He is *the* big-shot real estate operator up north of here, at least on the east side of the Hudson. He has had his own very successful real estate operation up there for years, and now he is even more powerful as the head of the Northland Realtors Association, which he rules like an iron-fisted dictator."

"Iron-fisted, eh? So noted. I will try to look more impressed. Please go on."

She drew in air and let it out, not softly. "Keller is a bloated and obnoxious windbag."

"So, should I put you down as undecided about him?"

That got a laugh. It was a pleasing laugh.

"All right," she replied, lifting her arms in surrender, palms toward me. "So I don't like the man. But then, over time, he has said some very nasty things about my husband."

"You have my attention."

"When Orson made it known—and made it known very clearly—that he was opposed to the so-called Northern Parkway, Keller began a smear campaign against him, suggesting that he was under the thumb of Franco Bacelli, the Mob boss. For instance, he called Orson a 'crime-syndicate toady' at a meeting of realtors up in Putnam County, and the comment got picked up by a local newspaper that had a reporter covering the meeting."

"I seem to remember that a couple of the New York dailies also glommed on to the quote," I put in. "But then didn't he—your husband—begin to change his position on the issue of the road?"

Elise shifted in her chair, pursing her lips. "Yes, he did . . . well, *alter* his stance somewhat. He allowed as to how there might be a way to shift the planned route of the parkway so as not to cut through . . . certain areas."

"Meaning in particular the estate of one Franco Bacelli?"

The color rose in her cheeks as she tensed up. "Orson knew that voters were beginning to drift away from him. His personal pollster, a strange little man named Keith Musgrove, told us that one canvass—this was about six weeks ago—showed that his popularity in the district had dropped by about seven percentage points since he had proposed the idea of an alternate route for the parkway. At that point, Musgrove became grim about his reelection chances."

"How did Bacelli like the new proposal?"

"Even though the road in the revised plan would still miss his estate by at least a half mile, he was damned angry and he let Orson know it. He felt that he had been betrayed."

"Not the kind of enemy most people would like to have," I observed.

Elise nodded. "And, of course, the original opponents of the project were even angrier than the Mob boss. They felt betrayed as well."

"You try to make everybody happy, and then you end up making nobody happy. Tell me about the anti-parkway crowd."

"Some of them, like Bacelli, have these sprawling properties, estates with horse farms, swimming pools, bridle paths, vineyards, forests, formal gardens, fountains, and the like. But there's also a group that calls itself CLEAN— 'Citizens Looking to Enjoy Arboreal Nature.' "

"Arboreal?"

She rolled her eyes. "I think that means trees and woods and countryside. Pretty hokey, isn't it?"

"Nero Wolfe would probably be able to rattle off at least three definitions of the word," I said. "I can guess just how this group must have felt about your late husband's switcheroo."

"They called Orson a turncoat and all sorts of nastier names. CLEAN's leader, an eccentric naturalist named Howell Baxter, branded him the most infamous traitor in the history of good old New York State since Benedict Arnold

41

sold out to the British in the Revolutionary War."

"Tough words. But for all the mudslinging over this road, it doesn't seem like there's a motive for murder here."

"Really? What about Bacelli, Archie? From what I know about the man, he's never been charged with murder, but chances are that he has ordered killings over the years, lots of them, don't you think?"

"I am not about to quarrel with you on that subject. The man is a lowlife, there's no question about it, but I can't see him orchestrating your husband's death. He's got his hands full right now fighting this hotshot young federal prosecutor who wants to make a name for himself by bagging the New York syndicate's big kahuna on a fistful of different charges.

"If half of what I read and hear from a highly placed friend at the *Gazette* is true," I continued, "Franco Bacelli has been forced into a defensive posture as the law begins to tighten the screws on him. He's got a lot bigger worries than some new road passing a half mile from his baronial homestead. If the Feds have their way, he may not even be able to enjoy that palatial estate of his much longer."

Elise DuVal folded her arms across her chest and raised her chin. "All right, Mr. Archie Goodwin, if you are correct in this assessment of Bacelli, just where does that leave us?"

I took a breath and prepared to jump into

deep water. "What should we know about Orson Milbank's personal life?" I asked.

The initial answer was a glare, followed by the silent mouthing of a word I choose not to repeat, followed by an attempt to stand. "I'm not going to stay and—"

"Sit, sit," I told Elise softly, placing a firm hand on her arm. "You came here to hire Nero Wolfe, and by extension me, to investigate your husband's death. If you are serious about finding the killer, as I certainly believe you are, then all avenues must be explored. Didn't the police ask you the same question I just did?"

"No, not at all," she said, squaring her shoulders. "They concentrated on the people and groups that have been for and against the parkway."

"Interesting. Well, I suppose one or more of those people might be tempted to commit murder if they felt the stakes were high enough. But, right now, I'm ranging more widely than our law enforcement representatives did. Talk to me."

Elise ran her tongue over her lips. "Well, I assume you know that I am Orson's second wife."

I nodded.

"His first wife is in a mental asylum someplace upstate," she went on. "They got divorced years before I met Orson. I've never laid eyes on her, but I know that neither of the children he had with her—a son, now in his late twenties, and a

43

daughter, a year or two younger—has anything to do with her."

"That's sad."

"Yes, it is, although for me, this is ancient history. Orson had put it behind him long before he and I got together."

"How do his children feel about you?"

She shrugged. "We—Mark and Irene and I— have always gotten along pretty well. I like to think they both came to realize that I have made their father happy."

"Happy enough that he wouldn't stray?"

"I suppose you've heard rumors?"

It was my turn to shrug. "This town is always full of rumors."

"As in Orson and Mona Fentress? I assume that is the direction where you're steering the conversation, Archie. Go ahead and say what's on your mind. I'm a big girl."

"Look, it gives me no pleasure to put the squeeze on you, but if we are going to push ahead with an investigation of Senator Milbank's death—and Mr. Wolfe will be the one to make that decision—then we have to have all the cards out on the table. I believe you understand that."

That got a nod from an unsmiling Elise. "All right," she said, her voice barely above a whisper. "Of course, I've heard talk about Mona and my husband. I got a snide comment from a neighbor of mine—not Lily Rowan, just so you know.

Anyway, I was at a benefit luncheon at the Plaza several weeks ago when this woman, whom I've never liked, came over to me and said 'Oh, Elise, it is ever so nice to see you again. I ran into Orson just last night at Toots Shor's. He was having dinner with that lovely assistant of his, the attractive blonde . . . oh dear, I just can't seem to think of her name.' Of course, she did know the name, Archie, but she wanted me to say it, so I did.

" 'Ah yes, Mona Fentress, what a lovely woman,' my neighbor purred. 'She's married to that Madison Avenue executive, isn't she? And our mutual acquaintance, Arlene Webster, was up in Albany a couple of weeks ago, and she saw Orson and Mrs. Fentress dancing in the ballroom at the Ten Eyck Hotel. Certainly, a small world, isn't it?' "

"Not very neighborly," I said. "Did you ever ask your husband about Mona Fentress?"

"Certainly, several times, even before I got approached at the Plaza by that catty gossip. Orson always laughed it off. 'Mona is absolutely invaluable to me,' he would say. 'She can charm newspaper reporters and editors, the governor, fellow senators, and constituents—even a lot of those who think I vote wrong. You don't have to worry about her. After all, she's got that handsome, wealthy husband who is minting money over on Madison Avenue.' "

"Did you believe him—about you not having to worry, I mean?"

"I am . . . not totally sure. You asked me to be honest, Archie, and I'm trying to. This is hard for me."

"I know it is, and I'm sorry—up to a point. Let me turn the question around: Did your husband have any reason to be suspicious of you?"

"In what way?"

"You tell me."

"To a large degree, we lived our own lives. Orson spent a lot of time in Albany. I joined him up there sometimes, but frankly, that town bored the daylights out of me. Hard to believe somebody made that burg the state capital way back when. I grew up in California, but I've long since learned that I'm a New York City girl through and through."

"But what if your husband had become a United States senator? I understand that was his goal."

"Move to Washington? Compared to Albany, I would have liked that, although maybe not as much as living in New York."

"Let's go back to my question: Did Orson Milbank have reason to be suspicious of you?"

"I was very fond of him, and I planned to stay married to him, Archie," Elise said. "That is all I care to say."

"All right, let's move on. You mentioned that Mona Fentress's husband has made big bucks over on Madison Avenue. I assume that means he's in the advertising business."

"It does. Although Charles Fentress is hardly

46

what you would call self-made. He hasn't earned all those big bucks himself. He owes his fortune almost entirely to his father, who cofounded the agency Powell and Fentress. The late Papa Fentress was a creative genius, or so I've been told. The son doesn't have half his brains, and he's arrogant and hot-tempered to boot."

"Are you speaking from experience?"

She nodded. "I've run into him a few times, and it's never been terribly pleasant. Once, he was particularly nasty to me."

"Go on."

"This was at a fund-raising dinner for Orson at a hotel up in White Plains. He and Mona were moving through the crowd, glad-handing supporters, and Charles came storming over to me in a foul mood. 'I wish you'd tell that husband of yours to stop working Mona so damned hard,' he snarled. 'I feel like I need an appointment to see her, for God's sake. I'm sick of it.'"

"A jealous husband talking?"

"I guess so, as well the liquor talking. He was more than just a little bit drunk. He ranted on loudly about how Orson was a slave driver until it seemed like everyone in the room was staring at us. I thought he was going to get violent until finally Mona came over, calmed him down, and led him away."

"Was that common behavior for him?"

"I later learned it was," Elise said. "He apparently flies off the handle a lot. Orson referred to him as having a 'short fuse.'"

"Interesting. Did you mention that episode to the police?"

She shook her head. "Fentress is a grown-up spoiled brat. He's apparently always angry about something, so at the time I didn't attach much significance to that outburst of his."

"Should I assume you don't see the advertising man as a murder suspect?"

"Yes, you should, surly as he is. Archie, I'm still sticking with Bacelli, despite your argument against it. The man is capable of anything, including hiring a sharpshooter and somehow sneaking him into a stadium."

"You may be right after all; I'm not about to argue the point. Let's get back to the baseball game. Had you been asked by your husband to be part of the group attending the game?"

"No, and as I said earlier, I was on my way up to Albany at the time because of that fund-raiser the next night. I was always picking and choosing the events that I attended with Orson. He thought I was good for his image, but that day at the game, Mona was going to be along, and she has more than enough glamour to go around," she said, an edge in her voice.

"Who were the others in the party?" I asked.

"Mona, of course. And let's see . . . there was Keith Musgrove, his pollster—"

"That 'strange little man' you mentioned earlier."

"Yes, and he is strange. Myopic and jittery. It made me nervous just being around him. Then there was Ross Davies, Orson's longtime campaign manager and speech writer, and Todd Armstrong, an intern just out of college who helped out wherever he was needed."

"Seems like that's a large staff for a state senator."

"It was, but Orson had big dreams," Elise said.

"So it would seem. Is there more I should know?"

"I can't think of anything at the moment. Do you think you can persuade your Mr. Wolfe to take me on as a client?"

"I can't make Nero Wolfe do anything he doesn't want to. For that, you need a miracle worker, which I'm sorry to say does not fall within my job description. But I'll go over everything you've said with him."

"Also, please give him this again, Archie," Elise said, squeezing my arm and handing me the check with all those zeroes that Wolfe had earlier rejected. "Maybe it will help."

"It sure can't hurt," I told her, grinning and placing the check under a paperweight on Wolfe's desk. "You'll be hearing from me."

CHAPTER 5

At lunch in the dining room, Wolfe and I attacked Fritz's broiled shad with sorrel sauce, which was worthy of attack. Wolfe does not discuss cases or prospective cases at meals, except in very rare instances. This apparently did not qualify as a rare instance. So while I continued to internally process my conversation with Elise DuVal between bites of the shad, Wolfe held forth on the impact of Charles Dickens's writings on the reforms made in England during the Industrial Revolution of the nineteenth century. As one who last read Dickens when I was in high school, and then only *Oliver Twist*, I mostly nodded and chewed.

Later, in the office with coffee, Wolfe spotted Elise's check on his desk and glared at it. "Well, report," he growled.

"Yes, sir." I proceeded to give him a verbatim account of my session with the one-time actress. He leaned back in his chair, interlaced his hands over his middle mound, and closed his eyes.

"So, Mr. Milbank's stance on the road had shifted," he remarked when I had finished. "It is a very hard undertaking to seek to please every-body."

"So I said to Elise DuVal."

"Not in those words, I am sure. They were spoken by Publilius Syrus in the first century before Christ."

"Okay, so now you're being picky," I told him.

"No, precise. Did you feel Miss DuVal to be truthful and forthcoming?"

Years ago, Wolfe got it into his head that I was an expert on women, and nothing I have said since to shake him from that conviction has had any effect.

"I think she believed everything she told me," I said. "Where she was not forthcoming, as I reported, was on the subject of any romantic life that she may have with someone other than the senator."

"Indeed? Your opinion?"

"I give three-to-one odds that she has had some, er . . . involvement outside of her marriage."

Wolfe nodded. "Just so. It has been some time since Mr. Cohen joined us for dinner. See if he is available tonight. Tell him we are having Cape Cod clam cakes, beef braised in red wine, squash with sour cream and dill, and avocado with watercress and black walnut kernels, followed by cherry tarts and, of course, that brandy he has often spoken of so highly."

This was a good sign. Lon Cohen is that "highly placed friend at the *Gazette*" I had mentioned to Elise DuVal. Wolfe and I had made use of Lon's encyclopedic knowledge of the city and its cast of characters countless times over the years, and he had been rewarded with equally countless scoops when Wolfe cracked a case. Lon does not have a title I'm aware of at the nation's fifth-largest newspaper, but he does have an office on the twentieth floor of the *Gazette* tower just two doors from the publisher's lavish suite.

"Good afternoon, oh noblest of ink-stained wretches," I said when he picked up his phone on the second ring. "I trust you are busy directing a vast army of reporters who are uncovering crime, corruption, and conspiracies both at home and abroad."

"And you, I presume, are, as usual, trying to find ways of justifying that princely salary Nero Wolfe pays you," Lon parried. "To what do I owe this interruption in my hectic schedule?"

"Mr. Wolfe has humbly requested your presence at dinner this evening on West Thirty-Fifth Street. The menu consists of Cape Cod clam cakes, beef braised in red wine, squash with sour cream and dill, avocado with watercress and black walnut kernels, et cetera, et cetera."

"I don't believe Nero Wolfe ever acts or speaks humbly. But I like all that I've heard about dinner, including those et ceteras. Anything special I need to do to prepare myself?"

"Just bring your brain. And, oh yes, I believe the word *brandy* may also have been mentioned."

"As in Remisier? For just a single bottle of that joyous elixir, I would sell my firstborn."

"We don't want your firstborn, we just want your soul," I told him. "See you at the usual time."

When the bell rang at seven o'clock, I swung the door open to Lon Cohen, lean, well dressed, shoes polished, black hair slicked down, and a thin smile on that dark, thoughtful face. If he was not the smartest newspaperman in New York, and maybe in the entire republic, I had yet to meet that individual. "Reporting as requested, Archie—and hungry as usual," he said, giving me a mock bow.

"Step inside, and we'll soon take care of the hungry part."

Fifteen minutes later, we were in the dining room sampling the Cape Cod clam cakes. Lon was itching to know what information Wolfe was looking for—that was invariably the reason for a dinner invite—but he well knew Wolfe's "no business talk at the table" policy, so he joined in the dinner conversation on whether the United States would use atomic bombs against North Korea. Wolfe said no, I said probably, and Lon sided with Wolfe, arguing that Harry Truman had presided over enough nuclear devastation after Hiroshima and Nagasaki.

Dinner behind us, we sat in the office with

coffee while Fritz poured brandy for Lon and me, receiving a broad grin and a nod of appreciation from our guest. "Mr. Cohen," Wolfe said, "I will ask a question I have posed to you on numerous occasions: Is it fair to say that in our past dealings, we have benefited more or less equally?"

"I would have to say that when you factor in the meals here—and the incomparable Remisier —I have probably gotten the better of the deal," Lon answered, raising his snifter in a salute.

The folds in Wolfe's cheeks deepened, which for him is a smile. "I am glad to hear that, for, once again, I am about to draw upon your storehouse of knowledge."

"By all means, draw away."

"A prospective client has asked me to investigate the murder at the Polo Grounds of Senator Orson Milbank."

Lon jerked upright in the red leather chair. "Well, I will be damned! When Archie called with the dinner invite, the first thing that occurred to me was that it had something to do with the Milbank shooting."

"You are perspicacious, sir. I have not yet accepted the commission, and I may not. To make a decision, I need more information."

"I'd love to know who your would-be client is, but I suppose that's off-limits for now," Lon said.

"You suppose correctly, although if I accept the

commission, you eventually will learn that person's identity."

"Now comes a question you no doubt were expecting: Will I also get a scoop?"

"I never make a promise I cannot keep, but that seems likely. Now for my second question of the evening: Was it widespread knowledge that Senator Milbank would be attending the baseball game on that fateful day?"

"Very much so," Lon said. "He has always been a strong proponent of citizens displaying the American flag at their businesses, homes, schools, and churches. He has even given flags free to his constituents who have requested them. And Milbank had made it known through his very efficient publicity mill that he would be attending the game on Flag Day—June 14—to underscore his great respect for the Stars and Stripes.

"One of our reporters learned that he had tried to get the Giants to let him throw out the first pitch. The team management said no, telling him they only give that honor to public officials who represent New York City, such as the governor or the mayor, the latter who often tosses out the first pitch on opening day in April."

"Was Mr. Milbank offended by this rebuff?" Wolfe asked.

"So we heard via the grapevine, but because he and his entourage already had purchased front-row box seats, the senator said they would attend the game, each of them carrying a flag. The Giants' organization had no objection to that. And why should they?"

"Archie, who was at the game, told me the senator and his cortege did indeed file into the stadium carrying and waving small flags," Wolfe said. "Am I correct in assuming it would have been easy for someone to possess advance knowledge that Mr. Milbank would be at this particular game?"

"Absolutely," Lon said. "The senator was an out-and-out publicity hound, and his office trumpeted the fact to the newspapers that he would be at the Polo Grounds—even where he would be sitting, so the press photographers would be able to spot him easily."

"Talk about a marked man," I put in. "Milbank might just as well have worn a bull's-eye."

Lon nodded while reaching for the Remisier at his elbow to refill his snifter. "Yeah, he made it ridiculously easy for anybody who wanted to get him. That's a big part of what's driving the police crazy, including no less than your old sparring partner Cramer."

Wolfe grunted. "Does the baseball team have any explanation as to how an individual with a rifle was able to get into their stadium unchallenged and apparently unnoticed?"

"They're falling all over themselves with excuses," Lon said. "The Giants claimed they were shorthanded on ushers and other employees that day, said there's a flu epidemic going around, which happens to be true, although they may be exaggerating the extent of the impact on their staffing. Besides, that lack of staffing was irrelevant in this instance because the outfield grandstands, where the police say the shot came from, are normally closed to paying customers on weekday afternoons and locked. However, we found out from the team's management that one gate to those outfield stands was found to be open after the shooting, and the lock had not been forced. The Giants insist that the gate had been locked the day before after a crew of electricians had been there to do some rewiring."

"Is it possible the electricians had neglected to lock the gate when they left?" Wolfe asked.

"Our man asked the Giants that very question," Lon replied, "but they claimed—and we have no reason to doubt them—that a watchman making his usual rounds the night before had checked all the gates around the periphery of the park. He found every one of them locked, including those that lead to the outfield grandstands."

"Okay, now let's see if I've got this straight," I said. "Somehow the shooter was able to get in, probably well before the game, and probably using some sort of key. He was toting a rifle, likely in some sort of case. He then climbed to the empty upper deck, where he shot Milbank dead from less than three hundred feet away—hardly a great distance for any half-decent marksman. Then it's probable that he slipped quickly out of the Polo Grounds during the ensuing chaos, not bothering to close the gate behind him."

"That would seem to sum it up, Archie," Lon said. "Sounds bizarre, I know. However, that appears to be the most plausible scenario."

"But where did the shooter get a key?" I asked.

"As he should have, our man posed that very question, and the stadium's head of maintenance had no answer. There are skeleton keys that open all the gates in the park, and he seemed vague as to whether they all are accounted for. He, our man, that is, got the impression that the maintenance department did not exercise much control about who had keys to those gates."

"No wonder Cramer's beside himself," I put in.

"Do your reporters or their sources have any insight as to a possible suspect?" Wolfe asked.

"Our guys hear all sorts of stories, some of which you may have picked up on. By far the most popular theory, not surprising, has Franco Bacelli behind the murder because Milbank had reneged on his total opposition to that parkway. Besides, the shooting has all the earmarks of a Mob hit."

Wolfe rang for beer. "Mr. Bacelli hardly ranks among nature's noblemen, to be sure, but would he be likely to kill a politician because of his stance on a highway, even a highway that might run near his home?"

"A fair question, and one I've been asking myself a lot lately," Lon said. "In the past, people who have defied him on even the most minor matters within the crime syndicate have ended up dead, or have simply disappeared, which also probably meant they were dead. The man is absolutely obsessive about defiance. Having said that, however, I find it difficult to believe he would order a killing over such a relatively trivial matter."

"Setting aside Franco Bacelli for the moment, who else might desire Mr. Milbank's death?"

Lon shrugged. "That is a tougher one. He had made enemies, to be sure. But had he made them angry enough to kill him?"

"What about others who had disagreed with the senator on the issue of that highway?"

"Jonah Keller, the real estate kingpin up north, is one tough customer, but offhand I don't see him behind a murder. Same with this bird Ray Corcoran, who heads up that Westchester–Putnam–Dutchess tri-county businessmen's group. They both were pushing damned hard for the parkway. They felt it was absolutely essential for the growth of their region."

"Would you agree?"

"I'm not so sure," Lon said, "but I can see where a strong argument could well be made for this high-speed divided parkway bringing more businesses—and more residents—to the area."

Wolfe poured beer and drained half a glass. "Would you say Mr. Milbank had enough power in the legislature to influence whether the road got built, and if so, its path?"

"He definitely does have that power, according to our Albany correspondent. Milbank had been in the senate a long time, and although he could be a pompous blowhard on occasion, he was one smart operator, and he worked to build up a lot of political capital among his fellow senators. He had voted for enough of their pet projects around the state that a majority of them would probably back him, although the issue had not yet come to a vote."

"Now that he is gone, what is likely to happen?" Wolfe posed.

"We are close enough to the November election that the Milbank seat will be left vacant until then. The man who was running against him, and who now seems likely to win the seat, is in favor of the road being built, and in its originally planned location. It remains to be seen who will replace Milbank on the ballot and what that candidate's position will be."

"So, would you say the real estate and business interests appear to have won the fight?"

Lon nodded. "Sounds to me like you're building a case for Keller or Corcoran as the murderer."

"Not necessarily. I merely make an observation," Wolfe said. "What of the individuals and organizations opposed to the road?"

"They are loud but mostly toothless, including that group calling itself CLEAN. Their best hope was Milbank, even given that he had backed down and proposed that alternate route. Although he waffled, I don't believe any of those people would have wanted him dead. They hardly seem to be the murdering types."

"What can you tell us about Mr. Milbank's private life?"

"Everything I hear from our man up north is that the senator was carrying on with his fetching press secretary, Mona Fentress," Lon said. "They had been seen all over both Manhattan and Albany, including coming out of the DeWitt Clinton Hotel in the capital early one morning. Very early."

"Maybe they were having a breakfast meeting," I said with a grin.

"And maybe I am the heir to the Rockefeller millions," Lon shot back. "Of course, Milbank wanted everyone—particularly his constituents—to think he and Mrs. Fentress were always together because they were planning strategy. You have to wonder, though, just how much strategy gets discussed on the dance floor or in the corner booth at a nightclub on the outskirts of Albany."

"The *Gazette* has eyes in many places," Wolfe observed.

"Yes, that's true," Lon said, "although we have never written a word about the Milbank–Fentress *situation*. I realize the press in this town does not always have a sterling reputation, but we, I'm speaking now only for the *Gazette*, are not about to print unproven accusations about a public figure's real or perceived extramarital activities."

"Were the spouses of those two suspicious of their relationship, Mr. Cohen?"

"I can't answer for Milbank's wife, the former movie actress who's rumored to have had a few flings of her own. But I do know that Mona's husband, the advertising executive Charles Fentress, has been heard in public growling about all the time his wife spends with the senator. One of our gossip columnists who seems to have ears everywhere says there have been a couple of dandy scenes in which Fentress has verbally ripped into his wife, although there are no reports that he ever attacked her physically."

Wolfe drew in a bushel of air and exhaled loudly. "Has he accused his wife of infidelity?"

"Not that we have heard, although heaven knows what he's said to her in private. I should point out that Fentress himself has somewhat of a reputation with the ladies. From what I've heard, his wife could level some of the same charges at him that he has fired off at her. "

"What a sweet bunch they all are," I put in. "So it seems both Milbanks and both Fentresses apparently like to shop around? Sounds like Charles Fentress is a first-class hypocrite."

"Along with being arrogant, generally obnoxious, and not overly bright," Lon said. "Story goes that he got into one of the Ivy League schools for two reasons: his famous father was an alumnus, and the younger Fentress's ability as a tennis player. He was ranked as the best tennis player among eastern universities two years in a row."

During Lon's recitation, Wolfe's face had registered various degrees of disgust. He had never taken a divorce case and surely never would, and although the subject of divorce did not arise during our conversation, we had definitely entered the realm of what Wolfe once termed *marital fragmentation*. However, when Lon concluded his recitation, Wolfe thanked him warmly. "As usual you have been most helpful," he said. "I would be appreciative of any other information relating to Mr. Milbank's death as your legions uncover it."

Lon chuckled. "Legions, eh? Sounds almost Roman. Any chance of naming your client? Not for print, of course."

"When I choose to divulge that information, it will be to the *Gazette*. On that you have my word."

"That is good enough for me. Well, this has been a most interesting evening, and for me one of the most gastronomically satisfying in months.

My compliments to Fritz." Lon got to his feet, and I walked him to the front door. "Just remember who your old buddy is when Wolfe cracks this baby," he said.

"He hasn't made a decision yet," I said, "so he may not do any cracking at all."

"Hah, so you say. I've got a sawbuck that says he'll take the case, all right, and deliver somebody to Inspector Cramer inside of two weeks."

When I returned to the office, Wolfe was pulling something out of his middle desk drawer. It was Elise DuVal's check with its many zeros. "Archie, deposit this in our account tomorrow morning. I will give you instructions at eleven."

"Yes, sir. As usual, your wish is my command." So Lon Cohen was barely down the front steps of the brownstone, and already he was half right.

CHAPTER 6

At seventeen minutes after nine the next morning, I stepped briskly out of the Midtown branch of the Continental Bank and Trust Company, having made one Lawrence S. Hopkinson very happy. For the record, the very prim and proper Mr. Hopkinson is a senior vice president at Continental who also likes to fancy himself as Nero Wolfe's personal banker. When I presented him with the DuVal check, I thought he was going to hug me, but he restrained himself, settling instead for an offer of coffee, which I politely declined. I had tasted the bank's coffee before.

Back in the office, I entered onto file cards the germination records that Theodore had brought down from the plant rooms earlier in the morning, although my mind was elsewhere. I was pleased that Wolfe had stirred himself to tackle the Milbank affair but disappointed that he hadn't given me marching orders either last night or first thing this morning while he was having breakfast in his bedroom. However, Nero Wolfe moves at his own speed, and experience long ago taught me I could rarely if ever accelerate that speed.

At one minute past eleven, I heard the hum of the elevator, and seconds later, Wolfe entered, placing orchids in the vase on his desk. After asking if I had slept well—I had—he eased into his chair and rang for beer.

"I have been to the bank," I told him. "Your dear friend Mr. Hopkinson sends you greetings and salutations. He was almost giddy when he saw the numbers on Miss DuVal's check."

"The gentleman may not be so solicitous if we soon withdraw the precise amount you deposited today," he remarked, pouring beer and watching the foam settle in the glass.

"Why in the world would we do that?"

"Archie, I have not yet decided to accept Mrs. Milbank—or Miss DuVal if you prefer—as a client."

"Well, you certainly acted like you were working when Lon Cohen was here last night. And it seems to me that by depositing that check today, you have committed yourself."

Wolfe narrowed his eyes. "I have committed to absolutely nothing."

"But last night, you said that I was to expect instructions this morning. I am ready," I told him.

"Do not badger me, confound it."

"All right, I won't. I will give you a choice instead: Either you take on Elise DuVal as a client, or I will. I mean it. You can grant me a leave of absence, or if that does not fit with your plans, I will resign and move out, giving you two weeks' notice, of course. I am told there's a very comfortable co-op building just three blocks east of here that has some vacancies, including a nice one-bedroom setup on the sixth floor. It goes without saying that I would miss Fritz's wonderful—"

"Flummery!"

"No, sir, not flummery. Back in the Dark Ages, I seem to recall that you hired me to be a man of action, a burr under your saddle. Well, I have not been seeing enough action lately, and when that happens, I get rusty. When I get rusty, I tend to get grouchy, and having two grouches under the same roof at the same time is a recipe for trouble."

"So you think I am grouchy?" Wolfe murmured, raising his eyebrows.

"I do indeed." He hates it when I use *indeed* because it's a favorite word of his. "Although you may have a fancier word than grouchy for that mood you so often find yourself in."

Wolfe began tracing circles with his right index finger on the arm of his chair, indicating that I had gotten to him. He was speechless for the moment, and damned angry to boot.

After two minutes of silence, Wolfe spoke. "All right, Mr. Goodwin, you want action, you will get it. Your notebook. What I am about to put forth would tax even your capacity to commit great amounts of detail to memory."

"Yes, sir."

For the next half hour, Wolfe piled on the instructions with relish, and in great detail. He was still sore that I had called him grouchy, but I didn't care. We appeared to have ourselves a case.

I tackled my easiest chore first—calling Elise DuVal. "You now are officially a client of Nero Wolfe," I told her.

"Wonderful, Archie! What do we do now?" she chirped. "I'm ready to take orders from you. I promise to be a good and obedient soldier."

"Excellent. First, you will say nothing about our arrangements to the police—absolutely nothing. They will find out soon enough about this, and they won't be happy."

"But shouldn't they know? It might make them work harder."

"Believe me, lady, the department is working plenty doggone hard as it is, many of the higher-ups probably damned near around the clock at this point. The newspapers, the mayor, and a passel of civic groups all are screaming at them, demanding action. For the moment, just sit tight and trust the brain of Mr. Wolfe. We will be giving you regular progress reports."

"But, Archie, I feel like I should be contributing something to the effort, other than money."

"I have a feeling that before this is over, you will have plenty of opportunities to contribute. For now, though, wait until you hear from us."

Elise held me on the line for another few minutes, asking all manner of questions about how we were going to proceed and begging me to let her help. I finally got rid of her by promising to telephone her often with progress reports.

My next task was to talk to Mona Fentress, whose husband was listed in the Manhattan directory at a Park Avenue address. To my surprise, the lady answered the telephone. When I introduced myself as Nero Wolfe's assistant, said we had been hired to investigate the senator's death, and asked if I could see her, the curt response was, "Why should I want to talk to you?"

"Why shouldn't you, Mrs. Fentress? So far, the police apparently haven't gotten anywhere in finding whoever shot your boss."

"They certainly haven't," she snapped. "What makes you and your Mr. Wolfe, famous as he is, believe that you can do any better than them?"

"Let me turn the question around: Could we do any worse?"

Silence at the other end. "I really don't see how I can help you," she finally said with a sigh, her voice now decidedly less aggressive.

"I honestly am not sure, but I don't see that you have anything to lose, other than an hour of your time or maybe even less," I said in what I hoped was my most persuasive tone.

"All right, if it can help find who did this thing," she said. "Where should I meet you?"

"You're not very far from Grand Central, I believe."

"Not at all, only about a ten-minute walk or a two-minute taxi ride, why?"

"There is a little café on the lower level of the terminal next to a same-day dry cleaners. The joint doesn't look like much, but they do have wonderful coffee, maybe the best you'll find in Midtown. Do you think you could be there in, say, twenty minutes or so?"

"Yes, but it would have to be for coffee only, not a meal. I've got a one o'clock lunch with a state assemblyman who may hire me to be on his staff."

"Well, that being the case, we certainly don't want to keep the gentleman waiting, do we?"

"No, even though it would be a comedown from a job with a senator. But I like to be working, particularly in the political world."

CHAPTER 7

Thirty minutes later, we sat in a back corner booth of the little joint with cups of coffee poured by an efficient but surly waitress. I had arrived a few minutes before Mona Fentress and had acclimated to darkness when she came in and peered around. I waved her over, noting that with her slender figure and flowing blonde hair, she looked every bit as much like a film actress as Elise DuVal.

"Thanks for coming," I said when she slid into the booth opposite me. "As I told you on the phone, I will not waste your time."

"At the moment, I have all sorts of time, Mr. Goodwin, other than today's lunch. At the risk of stating the obvious, my job has disappeared."

"Please call me Archie."

"I will, and I go by Mona to almost everyone. I seem to remember seeing your picture in the newspaper at one time, and Mr. Wolfe's, too. Probably a case the two of you solved."

"Make that a case Mr. Wolfe solved. I'm just his water boy and spear carrier."

"I doubt that very much . . . Archie. But I feel like I have seen you somewhere else, and recently."

"You have. Coincidentally, I was at the Polo Grounds on that afternoon, sitting just a few rows

71

away from your party. I was one of the people who rushed over, even before the police arrived."

She flinched. "It was all such a blur. You must not have stayed around for very long."

"I didn't. My friend and I were just onlookers who happened to be at that particular game. We would not have been good eyewitnesses, as we didn't see anything until after the senator was down."

"Did you and Nero Wolfe take the case because you had been there at the time?" she asked.

"No, Mona, we didn't. My being there was coincidental. We were approached by someone who has hired us."

"Who?"

"Sorry, but I can't tell you that, at least not now."

She sniffed and pulled out a cigarette, which I torched with my lighter. "So . . . you want to see if you can pry any information from me, but you're not forthcoming yourself, is that the situation we have?" she said between puffs, tilting her chin in a combative pose.

"I should think you would be glad Mr. Wolfe is working to learn who killed your boss," I told her, dodging the question.

"Oh, I am, Archie, truly I am," she said, softening her tone. "I'm sorry. It's just that I've been so distracted and so out of sorts ever since . . . what happened."

"Understandable, absolutely. Do you think you can go back over the events of that day at the ball park with me, or will it be too painful for you?"

"God knows I've relived it enough times already, particularly with the police, so I guess I can stand it one more time."

"Good, I appreciate that. First, tell me who was in your party at the game, and where they were sitting."

"There were five of us. Keith Musgrove, our pollster, had the seat on the aisle. Todd Armstrong, our young intern not long out of college at NYU, was on his right. He was helping me with press relations. Then came Orson, with me next to him, and on my right, Ross Davies, who was Orson's campaign manager and strategist."

"Good. Now let's take it from just before that Giant player, Reed Mason, hit the home run."

She ground out her barely smoked cigarette and took a sip of coffee. "As you know since you were there, it was a perfect day, and we all were enjoying ourselves. Because you were close by, you may have noticed that each of us carried a small American flag."

"Yeah, that was hard to miss."

"As you may be aware, Orson was known as a great flag lover. It pretty much had become his trademark, and this, you may remember, was Flag Day. As his press secretary, I was dead set against the flag business when he first got excited about it several years back. He even wanted to dub himself 'Mr. Stars and Stripes,' for Lord's sake.

"I felt the whole thing was incredibly hokey, and I tried several times to talk him out of it, without success. That just goes to show how badly I misread the pulse of his electorate. They loved it, and when he offered to give away American flags, dozens of people in the district, possibly as many as a hundred or more, took him up on it."

"That could get pretty costly."

"So you would certainly think, but not really," Mona said, taking another sip of her coffee. "He sweet-talked a flag-making outfit up around Mount Kisco into giving us a great deal on a bulk order, and we, in turn, made sure to credit the manufacturer to everyone who got a free flag. Their business boomed as a result, and everyone came out ahead. Honestly, there were times when Orson looked like an absolute genius. He even had a campaign called 'American flags make great Christmas gifts,' in which he urged people to buy flags from the Mount Kisco operation."

"Politics and the free-enterprise system working hand-in-hand," I said. "Let's get back to the game."

"Oh yes, sorry. Ever since . . . what happened, I tend to go off on tangents. All right, when the home run got hit, we all jumped to our feet and the spike heel on my right pump snapped off—they were damned expensive shoes, too, my favorites, which I had no business wearing to a baseball

74

stadium. Chalk it up to vanity. I tipped to my right, hitting the metal armrest and almost landing on Ross Davies, who was next to me on that side. And I have a vague recollection of Orson leaning over my other armrest and putting his arm around me to keep me from falling. Then . . . then he just collapsed, fell down across the two seats and against me. I know that I didn't hear gunfire or anything like that."

"You wouldn't have heard a shot with all the crowd noise around you, all of that cheering about the home run," I told her. "What do you remember next?"

"Pandemonium," she said, her hand shaking as she took out another cigarette, which I lit. "I sort of remember a short man with a big nose bending over Orson and putting a hand on his neck, on his—what—carotid artery?"

"That was my friend, the man I was sitting with. His name is Saul Panzer. He's a private investigator who sometimes does work for Nero Wolfe."

"Oh. The most horrible part was Orson's expression. His eyes were wide open, like he'd been surprised. Looking at him, it was hard to believe he was gone. I'll never forget that moment as long as I live."

"You said all of this to the police?"

She nodded. "Pretty much just the way I told it to you."

"All right, thanks for going through it again. I assume the police asked if you had any idea who might want to kill the senator."

"Yes. And I said my number one choice would be that Mafia bastard Franco Bacelli. After Orson modified his views on the route of the parkway, Bacelli starting calling him and making indirect threats."

"Such as?"

"He would phone Orson and say things like 'I hope you enjoy your last days in office,' or 'If things had worked out differently, you might have become governor or gone on to Washington.'"

"Maybe he said that because he assumed Senator Milbank was going to lose his upcoming election."

"No, Archie, I don't think that was the case. What Orson told me was that Bacelli sounded very threatening."

"Well, the guy has certainly issued his share of threats over the years, and he, through hit men, has followed through on a good many of those threats. Okay, anybody else that you'd like to nominate as possible killers?"

"There's Jonah Keller, the real estate kingpin up north. He is a loudmouth and a bully, and he's been determined to see the parkway built. Keller views the road as a personal crusade, a bonanza for that part of the state—and, of course, for all of the realtors up that way, too. He envisions the metropolitan area growing northward and feels the road will spur that growth, which may very well be the case. He has ripped into Orson in the press, calling him a lackey for special interests, particularly all of those wealthy landowners who want to keep the area 'underdeveloped,' to use Keller's term."

"Do you think the man is capable of orchestrating a murder?"

Mona gave a toss of her head. "Sure, why not? I've met the guy, and he's downright mean, there's no other word for it. And he's got a reputation for being ruthless in his business practices. Who's to say that ruthlessness wouldn't extend to violence?"

"What can you tell me about the other guy up in that region, the one who heads that trade group?"

"You're talking about Ray Corcoran, who runs the tri-county business association. He's a smooth operator, much more personable and amiable than Keller, at least on the surface. But he's said some tough things about Orson, too. Called him a 'barrier to progress' and 'one of the great minds of the nineteenth century.' Archie, I'm going to anticipate your next question and rank this trio in the order I suspect them of the murder: one, Bacelli; two, Keller; three, Corcoran."

"You've obviously given this some thought. Did you share your ranking with the police?"

"I did, Archie, and they nodded politely but didn't seem terribly interested in my opinion, although Inspector Cramer did take some notes." Her experience with the police sounded a lot like Elise DuVal's.

"Yeah, they can be that way; I've experienced it, too. I want to shift gears now. How would you describe your relationship with Orson Milbank?"

She studied the half-smoked cigarette in her hand for several seconds as if wondering how it got there, then looked up and gave me a tight smile. "Just what have you heard?"

"That the two of you worked together very closely."

"That is certainly true. What else?"

"Nothing I would consider to be credible information."

"A very diplomatic answer, Archie. What have you learned that you would tend to discredit?"

"Why don't you tell me that yourself, Mona."

"All right, I will. You have undoubtedly heard there was more than a professional relationship between us."

"I make a point to never believe everything I hear. As they say, talk is cheap."

"True, but, Archie, you must have suspicions or else you would not have raised the issue."

"All right, for purposes of discussion, let's say I may be suspicious—call it one of the occupational necessities of being a private detective."

Mona smiled tightly. "You're pretty glib, aren't you?"

"Maybe that's an occupational necessity, too. I've never thought of myself that way before."

"All right, enough of this repartee," she said. "May I tell you something in confidence?"

I held up a hand. "Be careful here, Mona. I keep confidences only as long as they don't have an effect on a case I'm involved in."

She laughed joylessly. "Oh, what does it matter now? I was in love with Orson, and he felt the same way about me. So there it is, out on the table. Is that what you wanted to hear?"

Wolfe is going to really hate this business, I thought. "Were your husband and Milbank's wife aware of this?"

"I can't speak for sure about Elise, but Charles certainly had an idea of what was going on. If you haven't gotten word about some of the public scenes we had, I'm surprised. You seem like a man who knows a great deal about what goes on in this city."

"All right, maybe I have heard rumblings."

"Rumblings—hah! With Charles, they were more like eruptions. The irony is that he had been playing around long before Orson and I got together. Ours has been a marriage in name only for years. Charles posing as the outraged husband is a classic study in phoniness."

"Which, of course, raises a question that an

intrepid private investigator is forced to ask: Could your husband have been behind the shooting?"

This time, Mona's laugh was hearty. "Oh God, no, Archie. Never. Charles growls, but, like a lot of yipping dogs, he has no bite. He can be mean and petty and insulting, no question, but deep down he's spineless and downright cowardly. Years ago, I got fooled by his looks and what then seemed like charm. And he also was a very good dancer, which always has impressed me—far too much in this case. Anyway, to finish answering your question, he could be called a lot of things that a newspaper can't print, but he is no killer. However," she said with what I would term an impish grin, "you've given me an idea. I'm going to have a little fun at Mr. Charles Fentress's expense over this situation."

"I am not sure I like the sound of that, Mona."

"Oh, don't be an old stick-in-the-mud, Archie," she said, waving a well-manicured hand in a dismissive gesture. "Charles can be so bloody pompous, and sometimes I just can't resist getting under his skin."

"Given the way the two of you seem to feel about each other, I'm curious as to why you didn't get divorced long ago."

"To be honest, the subject has come up between us several times, but Charles always fights the idea. He seems terrified that I'll take him for

80

everything he's got, which is ridiculous, and I've told him so more than once. For one thing, we have no children, so there would be no payments in that regard. For another, although my family is definitely not anywhere near as wealthy as the Fentresses, my own father, rest his dear soul, did okay on Wall Street once he survived the Depression, and he left me fairly well fixed. So there would not be an issue of alimony. I would be able to get along fine without Charles's money."

"Your husband's fortune comes from the advertising business, I understand."

"Yes, Darryl Fentress was considered a Madison Avenue creative genius, and after he died, Charles got willed half the agency, Powell and Fentress, even though he isn't anywhere near the advertising man his father was. I'm not even sure what he does there, other than glad-hand clients at long, martini-laced lunches at the priciest restaurants in Manhattan on his fat expense account. I'm sure that he's very good at that, anyway."

"So the plan is for the two of you to just keep going on the way you are indefinitely?"

A shrug and a sniff. "I guess so. Lately, I haven't done much thinking about the future. Anything else you need to ask, Archie?"

"No, I think that does it, at least for now, Mona. I appreciate the time you've given me."

"You are a good man, Archie," she said, hugging

me as we stood to leave. "And like the song says, 'A Good Man Is Hard to Find.'"

As I paid the check and Mona walked out of the little café with a glance over her shoulder and a wave, I wondered if she would someday find herself that elusive good man.

CHAPTER 8

I got back to the brownstone just in time to sit down to lunch—veal cutlets along with Fritz's mixed salad with Devil's Rain dressing and capped off with a cherry tart. As we ate, I listened to Wolfe's monologue on why broadcast news is so shallow and superficial and waited until we were in the office with coffee to fill him in on my session with Mona Fentress.

After I finished reporting, Wolfe made no comment, turning instead to an orchid catalog that had arrived in the morning mail. "So . . . do you have any thoughts on Mrs. Fentress?" I asked.

"None whatever," he said as he leafed through the catalog.

"Am I boring you? Or perhaps you are disappointed that I didn't throw more probing questions at the lady. Maybe you can give me a list of things to ask, and I can set up another coffee date with her. I'm always eager to improve my interviewing technique, and I'd be glad to—"

"Archie, shut up!"

"Yes, sir. If you have no further instructions for me, I'll just mosey up to my room and polish my shoes. I noticed today that my brown ones are scuffed on the right toe and the black pair could use a good buffing." As I walked out of the office, Wolfe's nose was still buried in the catalog, and my blood pressure was rising.

It is not unusual during a case for Wolfe to suffer a relapse and quit working altogether, but these spells usually occurred when an investigation was further along, and this one had barely gotten under way. I've lived through numerous relapses over the years and have yet to figure out what triggers them or how to end them. Some last less than a day while others go on for a week or more. The symptoms vary, but most often they involve eating, lots of eating. For instance, during one such episode, Wolfe consumed half a sheep in two days, with different parts of the animal cooked twenty different ways. During these spells, when he is not eating prodigious amounts, he either takes to his bed or sits on a stool in the kitchen driving Fritz to distraction with his dictates on precisely how dishes should—and should not—be prepared.

It was still too early to tell if this was a full-fledged relapse or simply an aversion to work that might quickly pass. But taking no chances, I went to the kitchen to alert Fritz. He shook his head and frowned. "Archie, you are right. The signs are there. When you were away before lunch, he came into the kitchen and stood over me as I prepared the cutlets and kept insisting that I must use dried oregano leaves instead of powdered oregano."

"Did you poke him in the eye with a fork?"

"No, Archie, I would never do such a thing— Oh, you are making a joke," Fritz said, looking slightly chagrined. "But I did become somewhat angry, and he finally agreed to let me use the powdered oregano. I just hope that this afternoon he doesn't tell me how to make my Brazilian lobster salad."

"That's the dinner entrée?" I asked. Fritz nodded.

"Darn, a favorite of mine," I said. "I'm going to be away until well past dinnertime. Would you save me some?" Fritz said he would.

Although Wolfe had apparently opted to sit on the sidelines for now, I still had the assignments he had given me earlier, back when he was pretending to work. Among those chores were visits to Jonah Keller, Ray Corcoran, and Howell Baxter up north of the city. I was sorry to stick Fritz with Wolfe in his present state but happy to be away from the brownstone for much of the day.

Keller's office was in White Plains, while Corcoran had his farther north in Carmel. Baxter, the head of Citizens Looking to Enjoy Arboreal Nature, or CLEAN, operated out of his home in Wappingers Falls. I armed myself with their addresses, and this being one of those perfect June afternoons, the kind poets rhapsodize about, I took the convertible rather than the Heron sedan from Curran's Motors on Tenth Avenue, where Wolfe has garaged his cars for years.

Within minutes, I was breaking the speed limit on the Henry Hudson Parkway, along with almost every other car heading north. Nothing improves my mood more than being behind the wheel on a fine day with only sky above me, and by the time I had angled east onto the Bronx River Parkway and entered White Plains, I was at peace with the world.

I double-checked the address of the Northland Realtors Association, of which Jonah Keller was chairman, and had no trouble finding the building, a three-story redbrick American Colonial structure with white-shuttered windows near the downtown district. It was fronted by an elm-shaded lawn with grass that looked like it had been lifted from the putting green at an exclusive country club.

Inside, the reception area sent a clear message that recent times had been very good indeed for the real estate industry in this part of the state. Plush carpeting, gleaming brass chandeliers, paneled walls with framed landscape paintings, upholstered chairs, and ivory draperies made me feel like I had stepped into the spacious lobby of a three-star hotel.

Seated behind a half-acre of glistening, glass-topped mahogany, a perky young brunette whose desk plaque read ARLENE WILLIS flashed me a smile that showed off her dimples. "May I help you, sir?" she said breathlessly.

"Yes, I would like to see Mr. Keller."

"Is he expecting you, sir?"

When I said no, she gave me a little-girl frown and fed me the obviously rehearsed line that he was in conference and probably would be for some time—maybe all afternoon.

"Oh, that is too bad, Miss Willis. I really had hoped to see him. Do you think you could get a message to him?" I asked, giving her a smile of my own, one that Lily Rowan had told me was deceptively disarming.

Arlene batted her brown eyes. "What is the message, sir?"

"Let me write it down; it is rather personal and very important," I said, scribbling a sentence on the back of one of my business cards. "Do you have an envelope I might use?"

She frowned again and opened a desk drawer, pulling out an envelope and handing it to me. I slipped my card in, sealed the flap, and wrote Keller's name on the front. "Would you see that he gets it now, please?"

"I will try, sir," she said, getting up and opening a door several paces behind her. She disappeared and was gone for two minutes. On returning, she soberly reported, "Mr. Keller will be out to see you momentarily, sir."

The "momentarily" became closer to ten minutes. I was prepared for an angry Jonah Keller, and he did not disappoint. Stocky and florid, the man looked like he could have had smoke coming out of both ears. "You!" he barked, "Come with me." As the ever-so-proper Arlene watched with a furrowed forehead, I followed Keller through a doorway and into a windowless conference room with a round table, four leather chairs, a few framed paintings of mountains and lakes, and a brass chandelier, which looked like a smaller version of the ones in the lobby.

He closed the door and tossed my business card down on the table. "What in the hell is the meaning of this, Goodwin?" he barked, tugging on the points of his overtaxed vest.

"I thought it was self-explanatory," I replied blandly, picking up my card. "Did I misspell any of the words? Let's see . . . no, everything appears to be in order, and I like to think my handwriting is legible. Way back when I learned on the Palmer Method, I always got good grades in penmanship at school. In case you had trouble reading it, here's what I wrote: 'I need to talk to you about a murder.' "

"I know damn well what you wrote," Keller snapped, slapping a fleshy hand down on the tabletop. "But I don't have the foggiest idea what in God's name you are talking about."

"Sorry I wasn't clearer. I am talking about the shooting of Senator Orson Milbank," I replied, keeping my tone bland.

"Yeah, so? Why do you need to talk to me? By

the way, Goodwin, I know who you are, in case you believe we're a bunch of out-of-touch yokels up here in what you think of as the sticks. You work for that fat so-called genius down in Manhattan, Nero Wolfe."

"Oh dear, Mr. Wolfe would not like the 'so-called' part. Anyway, we understand you were far from friendly with Senator Milbank."

"That's right. And just what of it?" he said, folding beefy arms across his chest.

"Mr. Wolfe has been hired to find out who is behind the senator's death, and he felt you might be able to give us some insights."

Keller made a sound somewhere between a laugh and a growl. "So . . . he thinks I had something to do with Milbank's killing, is that it?"

"Not necessarily, he—"

"I am offended, deeply offended," he huffed, trying without success to square rounded shoulders. "Maybe you are not aware of this, Goodwin, but I am one of the best-known, most respected people in this entire county, and in the surrounding counties, for that matter. My name means something here. I could sue you—and your fat boss—for slander."

"Why? No one has accused you of anything, Mr. Keller, other than being well plugged into what goes on in this area."

"Goddammit, it's the implication! Now, it's

hardly a secret that I had no love for Orson Milbank, but if I went around killing everyone I didn't like, I would have a dead brother-in-law, a dead IRS auditor, and a dead local physician, who shall remain nameless. And by the way, shamus, you're late to the party. I have already had a visit from a lieutenant named Lawson from the New York Police Department Homicide Squad."

"What did he ask you?"

"None of your damned business!" Keller shouted, giving me a hard shove in the chest with his palm. I wasn't expecting it and went back on my heels as he shoved me a second time. I sidestepped him, spun him around, and got his fat right arm in a hammerlock.

"Hardly a very nice way to treat a guest," I said, forcing the arm up as Keller groaned.

"Not an invited guest," he spit out between groans, along with a couple of other words.

"True, but nonetheless, it isn't neighborly," I said, releasing him.

Keller rubbed his arm and scowled. "You lay a hand on me again, Goodwin, and by God, I'll call a guard to have you thrown out. Now, I have better things to do than talk to some sleazy New York gumshoe. That's what they call you guys, isn't it—gumshoes? I believe you know the way out. Don't linger." With that, the self-styled real estate kingpin of three counties stormed from the room, leaving the door open behind him.

"Nice to have met you," I said to Arlene Willis as I passed her desk. "Keep up the good work here. You're doing an outstanding job."

"Thank you, sir. I certainly will try my best. I hope you have a fine rest of the day, sir," she pronounced.

"I will, in large part thanks to the memory of your wonderful smile," I told her as the color rose in her cheeks. I departed having made one person in that office happy.

CHAPTER 9

So I had not endeared myself to Jonah Keller, but I wasn't sure any approach would have worked on him other than one that would feed his outsized ego. As I wound north through the rolling hills and reservoir country to Carmel, I thought about how to figuratively tackle Ray Corcoran of the Westchester–Putnam–Dutchess Business Association. One thing was sure: I would not send him a business card with *murder* written anywhere on it.

When I hit the outskirts of Carmel, I pulled into a filling station to gas up and get directions. I showed the lanky attendant the address, and he nodded, running a grease-stained hand over his unshaven cheek. "Oh sure, that's Mr. Corcoran's office. Just stay on this road; it's less than a mile ahead on the left. You can't miss the place, a brown-brick building with a red awning. Mac's Barbershop is on one side of it and Belle's Tip-Top Restaurant on the other."

After paying and thanking him, I prepared to drive off. "Appreciate your business, sir," he said. "That Mr. Corcoran who you're heading off to see is one fine gent, I'm here to tell ya. Been buyin' his gas and oil here for years, 'cept, 'course, when he was off to the war. Always asks about the wife and kids, and how business is."

"And how is business?" I asked, to be sociable.

"Pretty doggone good," he said with a grin. "And that's partly 'cause of Mr. Corcoran. He's made sure that I'm the only one for miles around that carries this brand." He pointed to the colorful oil company logo on the post above us. Driving into Carmel, I wondered how—and why—Ray Corcoran had allowed the gas station operator to have a monopoly of sorts.

White Plains seemed like a metropolis compared with Carmel, although the main drag of this little Putnam County burg could have provided a fitting backdrop for a Norman Rockwell painting. I found the one-story brick building between the barbershop and Belle's restaurant with no trouble. The sign painted on the glass of the front window proclaimed it to be the WESTCHESTER-PUTNAM-DUTCHESS BUSINESS ASSOCIATION, ALWAYS LOOKING TO THE FUTURE, RAYMOND L. CORCORAN, EXECUTIVE DIRECTOR.

I stepped into a carpeted reception area and found myself looking at the cheerful face of a white-haired lady with rimless glasses. "Welcome, sir," she said as if she meant it. "How may I help you?" Her smile would have melted the heart of a process server.

I gave her my name and asked to see Corcoran. When she asked about the nature of my business, I told her it was somewhat personal.

"Well, Mr. Corcoran should be back in . . . oh, about twenty minutes, if you would care to wait. He's in a meeting just down the street at the VFW hall. Can I get you coffee?"

I declined with thanks and sat in one of the three guest chairs reading a three-week-old issue of the *Saturday Evening Post*—with a painting by Rockwell, no less, of boys frolicking at a swimming hole on the cover. As I was finishing my second pass through the magazine, a well-turned-out man of medium height who looked to be in his late thirties stepped in from the street, looked at me with raised eyebrows, then turned to his receptionist with a quizzical expression.

"This gentleman, his name is Goodwin, asked to see you," she said.

"What can I do for you, sir?" Ray Corcoran asked in a neutral tone.

"My name is Archie Goodwin, and I would like to take a few minutes of your time. I assure you that I am not selling anything, nor am I looking for money or a job, or a favor of any kind."

"Hmm, I suppose you're harmless enough then," he said with a grin. "Come on into my office, Mr. Goodwin." I followed him through a doorway and into a large corner room that looked out onto a tree-shaded, parklike area with swings, a slide, a seesaw, and a baseball diamond with a wire-mesh backstop and some wooden bleachers. Corcoran gestured me to a guest chair and slid in behind his desk, leaning back and cupping his hands behind his head. The wall behind him was filled with certificates from various civic organizations, plus a brass plaque with two small American flags pinned above it.

"That's very nice," I observed, pointing to the plaque.

"Oh, thanks," he said. "I got that from our local VFW for volunteer work I've done for them over the years. A great organization, wonderful people. I'm a veteran myself, marines, and saw some active duty in the Pacific, on a God-forsaken island called Tarawa, you may have heard of it."

"Of course I did, one of the bloodiest battles of the war. Three days of fighting, weren't there?"

"Yes, but it seemed like three weeks. You seem up on the campaign. Did you serve?"

"Only stateside, Washington, with the army. I was a major," I said. "Although I never felt I deserved the rank."

"Nonsense! If you were given a commission, of course you deserved it," Corcoran said. "I was promoted to major myself, near the end of the war, so we have something in common." He paused and wrinkled his brow. "Archie Goodwin. That name sounds somehow familiar. Why do I recognize it?" he asked cordially.

"I work for the detective Nero Wolfe."

"Of course, that's it!" he said, coming forward, grinning and clapping his hands once. He ran a palm over well-barbered light brown hair. "I've believe I've seen your name in the New York papers a few times. To what do I owe this visit?"

"My boss has been hired to investigate the shooting of your state senator."

His smile was replaced with a look of concern. "It was a terrible thing that happened, outrageous," he said solemnly, giving his necktie a tug. "I was definitely not one of Orson Milbank's supporters, Mr. Goodwin, but I always felt that he took his job very seriously, and I admire that in any man, whether I agree with everything he says or not. In fact, those two small flags on either side of my VFW award came from Orson. He was always passing out flags, large and small. He donated the big flag that hangs in our VFW hall down the street from here, where I just had a meeting to plan our annual picnic for disabled veterans."

I nodded. "I understand you were among those who strongly opposed the senator's position on the building of a parkway that would connect this area with New York City."

Corcoran nodded. "That is no secret, of course, Mr. Goodwin. I—as well as our entire association and many other civic leaders—have been a strong supporter of the Northern Parkway project, which we feel is absolutely vital to the growth and prosperity of our three-county area if we are to continue to grow, develop, and prosper. Orson felt otherwise, as you know."

"But I understand that he recently had backed off at least to a degree on his opposition to the road."

"That is correct, sir. And at the risk of ascribing motives, I feel that he shifted because of his concern over the fall election. Many people in this part of the state believe as our association does—that the future lies in the private automobile. Already in the few years since the end of the war, all across the country new four-lane highways, many of them divided by medians and with limited access, have been built, and many more are on the drawing boards from coast to coast. This is the beginning of a new era, and we up here simply cannot afford to be left behind our brethren here and in other states."

"What do you see as the benefits of a Northern Parkway?"

"Where to start?" Corcoran asked, spreading his arms, palms up. "New businesses, factories, housing developments, retail centers, schools, you name it. Some areas of our three fine counties have languished as a backwater because of a sadly outdated system of roads, many of which have been in place for a half century or even longer. A lot of these roads were built in the horse-and-buggy era and look like it. The new parkway will rapidly change all of that."

"Any chance the presumed influx of people also will bring new businesses that could harm local enterprises in the process?"

His hands formed a chapel. "Mm, no, we are very careful about protecting existing members of our association. We always have been." *Like the gas station operator,* I thought.

"What do you think of the theory that Franco Bacelli orchestrated the senator's death?"

"Good Lord! I couldn't possibly comment on such an accusation," Corcoran said, jerking upright and looking shocked.

"Mr. Corcoran, in your position, you must know a great deal about what goes on in this corner of the world," I told him. "Do you have any thoughts as to a possible suspect?"

He studied a cufflink, then steepled his fingers again and frowned. "No, there isn't anyone who I could even conceive of doing such a thing, Mr. Goodwin. Not a soul. We have an extremely low crime rate here, as you probably know. Nothing like your Manhattan, no offense intended."

"None taken. How did you and your association feel about Senator Milbank's proposed alternate route for the parkway?"

"Frankly and candidly, we did not think much of it," he said, frowning. "The route we envisioned was ideal, in that it entered or came very close to the maximum number of the larger population centers throughout the three-county area. The senator's proposed route, on the other hand, was much less convenient to several of our bigger communities."

"You've been pretty tough on Milbank from what I hear. You have said he was a barrier to progress and called him 'one of the great minds of the nineteenth century,' right?"

That got a chuckle from Corcoran. "Oh, sometimes I suppose we do things for effect," he said with a shrug. "I believe that was among the quotes I gave to one of the local newspapers about Orson. I wouldn't take that too seriously. I don't believe he did. After all, as a politician, he tossed off a lot of comments about opponents during campaigns that were for effect as well."

"What do you think of that group calling itself CLEAN?"

Corcoran waved a hand dismissively and snorted. "They're a weird bunch, always harping on the fact that we need to keep all of our open spaces. This despite the fact that we already are blessed with award-winning park systems and forest preserves within our boundaries, to say nothing of several popular state parks. No, these folks want to return to the days when those first Dutch settlers put down their roots around here more than three centuries ago. They challenge every single building project or new road that gets proposed."

"What do you think of the guy who runs CLEAN?"

Another snort from Corcoran, along with an indulgent chuckle. "Howell Baxter? Oh, he's a fanatic; I don't know what else to call him. In his ideal world, this area would be filled only with a few settlers living in log cabins and a tribe or two of Indians hunting with bows and arrows. In fact, I have it on good authority that Baxter actually lives in a log cabin himself, although I have never seen it." Another chuckle, this one derisive.

"I gather Mr. Baxter and his group weren't very happy with Milbank when the senator suggested a compromise route."

"They sure as heck weren't. Baxter, who up to that point had seemed to be so buddy-buddy with Orson, began to call him all sorts of names in print. From my perspective, the man is absolutely impossible to please."

"Would he have been angry enough to want Milbank dead?"

"Oh, now I would never go that far, Mr. Goodwin," Corcoran said, holding up a hand. "After all, among other things, Howell Baxter claims to be a pacifist."

"Just an often angry pacifist, it seems."

"I'll say. Well, is there anything else I can help you with?"

"I don't think so, Mr. Corcoran. I appreciate your time."

"Not at all, Mr. Goodwin, not at all," he said, standing and holding out a paw, which I shook. "Very nice to have met you. When you came in

100

here, I actually thought for a minute that you might be sizing me up as a possible suspect. Silly, isn't it?"

"Very silly, indeed," I agreed, rising to leave.

CHAPTER 10

I left Carmel and the ever-so-upright Raymond L. Corcoran in my wake and undertook the third and longest leg of my fact-finding expedition, this one north to Wappingers Falls in Dutchess County. The drive proved a scenic one, through rolling hills and past farm fields and pastures filled with black-and-white cows, red barns, and green tractors. It looked a lot like the Ohio countryside where I grew up. The last leg took me up Route 9 a little east of the Hudson, and just after I passed the WELCOME TO HISTORIC WAPPINGERS FALLS sign, I pulled up in front of a small roadside grocery to get directions.

"Ah, so you're gonna see old Howell, are you now?" said the wizened little lady behind the counter who wore a soiled apron and had a pencil behind one ear. "He's gotta be dern near as old as me, although I ain't never been able to get him to tell his age. Which is all right, because I won't tell him mine, neither," she cackled. "He comes in, oh, three, four times a week for one thing and another. I think it's because he mainly likes to argue with me—about doggone near anything. If I say it looks like rain, he says no, it'll be sunny all day. If I say Jack Benny was funny on the radio the other night, he'll tell me how lousy he thought the show was. Howell's contrary and cantankerous, but I have to say I like him anyhow. He sort of grows on you, you know?"

I said I knew. "So his house is about a half mile ahead, on the right?"

"Easy to see," she said. "You'd be blind to miss it. Log-cabin type of place it is, perched up on a little rise above the road. Bet you're gonna talk to him about that rabble-rousing outfit of his, right?"

"You mean CLEAN?" I asked.

"Yeah, that's his passion, you might say. Howell, he don't like change, not one bit. I don't much like it myself, so leastways there's something that the two of us agreed on."

"How do you feel about your senator getting shot?"

She spread her arms, palms up. "I liked him well enough when he was against that doggone road they plan to build, but then he got kinda weak in the knees and started to chicken out, as maybe you heard."

"I did. Do you think that's why he was killed?"

"Nah, I think it had to do with women somehow. Talk in these parts for a long time has been that he liked the ladies at lot, so maybe it was some jealous husband. We had one of them deals here a few years back. Guy from over in Poughkeepsie was making time with the wife of a local jewelry store owner who caught 'em together in the middle of . . . well, I think you get the picture. Anyway, he shot the Poughkeepsie man dead, right there in the bedroom of his own doggone house not a half mile from here."

"What happened to the jeweler?" I asked.

"Went free," she said, slapping a palm on the counter and cackling again. "Justifiable homicide, they called it. Then he kicked his wife out, and she's never been seen in these parts since."

"Interesting story. Well, I'll be off. Thanks for the directions."

"As I said, you can't miss Howell's place. Oh, I almost forgot. Tell him that Nellie—that's me—says she just got some nice T-bones in. Howell loves his steaks, and I'll set one aside for him, but only if he comes by to get it tomorrow. After that, tell him I'll sell it to whoever drops in. As I said, I like Howell, but he knows dern well that I've got me a business to run, and times are tough, as I'm sure you know. Being neighborly goes only so far, doesn't it?"

I told her it did, and that I would pass along the message. I drove north until I saw the log cabin, sitting on a knoll just back from the road, as Nellie had described. I steered up the steep gravel drive to the front door, and as I engaged the emergency brake, a lean man with salt-and-pepper hair and a neatly trimmed beard showed himself in the doorway. "Nice wheels you got there, son," he said as I climbed out. "Bet that buggy had to cost you a dandy piece of change."

"That it did, all right. May I assume you are Howell Baxter?"

"Assume all that you want to, son. Just what brings you to this small corner of our fair state?"

Before I could answer, Baxter invited me in. "Just brewed a fresh pot of coffee. Do you drink the stuff?"

I said I did and was led into a large room with a timber-beamed ceiling, hardwood floor, woolen rugs with colorful geometric patterns, and shellacked log walls bearing a lot of Indian artifacts, including a feathered headdress, tomahawks, and oil portraits of tribal chiefs and teepees. I almost felt like I was in some sort of museum.

"I like this room," I told Baxter as he gestured me toward a chair made partly of logs and handed me a mug of steaming black coffee. I sat.

"It's okay, I guess," he answered. "Suits my needs just fine, has for years. Now what's your story, lad?"

I began to tell him who I was and how I happened to be in his small corner of this fair state, to use his phrase. Before I could finish, he broke into a sly grin.

"So, Archie Goodwin of New York City, you are really here because you and your boss— what's his name, Nero Wolfe?—think I was behind the killing of one Orson D. Milbank, Senator." His grin yielded to a dry but hearty laugh. "By damn, I like it! Yes sirree, I really do like it! Makes me feel dangerous, intriguing. I haven't felt dangerous in what?—forty years—back when I was still young enough to chase women, not that I ever caught any of them very often." Baxter laughed again, this time so hard that it morphed into a cough. When he recovered, he drank coffee, and before he could say anything more, I cut in.

"Mr. Baxter, please let me be clear. No one who I am aware of, least of all Nero Wolfe, is accusing you of anything. As I started to say before, because of your involvement in the Northern Parkway issue, we thought you could possibly have some thoughts about who might wish the senator ill."

He nodded, pursing his lips. "My own relations with Orson were, shall we say . . . uneven. But before I get into that, I gather you know at least a little something about our organization."

"I don't know a lot, but I am aware that CLEAN wants to keep this part of the state as unspoiled as possible."

"True, as far as it goes," Baxter said. "We are not a large group by any means, every one of them volunteers except me, and the only money I get is from folks kind enough to send checks and cash to support our work. And believe me, that's not a lot, welcome as it is.

"Some of my volunteers are coeds from Vassar,

over there in Poughkeepsie, nice, eager young women hoping they can help change the world for the better, even in a small way. A bunch of the girls helped me picket to stop a new county road from being built that would have sliced through one of our local parks, cutting it darn near in half. We got us some local newspaper and radio coverage, and by George, we won that one." He slapped a hand on his knee for emphasis.

"Now I know very well that a lot of folks hereabouts see me as an eccentric and maybe even deranged old coot who lives in the past. Now I allow that there is some truth to that—at least the old coot part—but I feel it's danged important to preserve our heritage up here. This very place was named for a local Indian tribe, the Wappingers. I'll bet one thin dime you did not know that."

"You're right, Mr. Baxter. I didn't."

"Anyhow, this abomination of a parkway that everybody's talking about is totally, absolutely unnecessary," he said, banging his fist down on a lamp table, causing a dog, a German shepherd I hadn't noticed before, to sit up from a nap in a far corner of the room and yawn before settling back to sleep.

"It's simply a creation of the commercial and real estate interests to draw more people up here," Baxter went on. "They want to open up the area to new housing developments, which will mean more people—more residents to patronize their businesses, which will, these interests hope, also mean new businesses and new industries as well. It will totally change the character of the region."

"And you feel this is not a good thing?"

"It sure as shootin' isn't, young Mr. Goodwin. The open spaces, except for a few parks here and there, would gradually disappear, and eventually you'd see the whole danged county paved over and turned into one gigantic suburb of your great and splendid city to the south. Trees would come down by the hundreds and farms would get sold off and their land turned into tracts with blocks lined with identical houses, just like what's already happened in other places, some of those places doggone close to here."

"You don't paint a very pretty picture, Mr. Baxter."

"Well, by heaven, it's not a very pretty picture," he said, leaning forward. "Back to Orson Milbank and our relationship: That's why you're here. I never figured him as a dedicated naturalist, but I did like the fact that he opposed the new parkway, even if he might have had some political or personal reasons for his position."

"Like maybe to curry favor with one Franco Bacelli?"

Baxter laughed and slapped his thigh. "I think I like you, city boy. You cut through all the bull and get right to the point."

"I wasn't always a city boy, back in Ohio."

"Good, I mighta known it. You still got some of the country in you, all right. It shows. Yeah, no question in my mind that Milbank was getting bankrolled at least to some degree by Bacelli and repaid him by objecting to the road, which would run too doggone close to that hoodlum's princely estate. At that time, the senator was doing the right thing for the wrong reason."

"But then . . . ?"

"But then, as I'm sure that a bright fella like you has figured out by now, Orson began to get worried about the November election. He was getting a lot of heat from people like that bloodsucking real estate devil Jonah Keller and his slick accomplice, Corcoran, the so-called 'businessman's friend.' They both hammered on the senator as an impediment to progress, and the local papers went right along with them like a bunch of lemmings blindly jumping off a cliff. The polls I read or heard about showed Milbank trailing the guy who figured to run against him in the fall."

I liked hearing the man pontificate, and I encouraged him to continue with a nod and a smile.

"So, the senator did what he felt he had to," Baxter went on between sips of coffee. "He 'modified' his position, that's the word he used in a statement—'modified.' All of a sudden, he magically came up with an alternate route for the parkway, one that might please at least a few in the business community and maybe, just maybe, would save Milbank his seat in that august group that decides our fate in that ugly pile of stone up in Albany that they call our capitol."

"But in the process, he got Bacelli all riled up," I said.

"That he did. And he got me all riled up, too, Archie Goodwin."

"Were you riled up enough to take some action against Mr. Milbank?"

That brought a grin. "You should know that I'm a pacifist, always have been. In the Great War, or World War I, as your generation of young bucks calls it now, I was a CO—that stands for 'conscientious objector.' Just check the records if you don't believe me. I wouldn't fight, but I was given the option of doing some other service, and I ended up working at a mental hospital down in Virginia during the war."

"So I should assume being a pacifist precludes bumping someone off—or hiring someone else to do the bumping off?"

"You just don't want to let loose of that bone, do you?" Baxter said, his grin still in place. "Even if I had wanted to kill Orson Milbank—which I didn't—I never would have considered such a thing. It's not in me."

"Is there anybody else who you would like to nominate as the one behind the killing?"

Baxter threw up a gnarled hand. "Not really. Oh, I suppose somewhere along the way, Bacelli will find himself dead center in the spotlight if he isn't already there. From what little I read in those big city papers you've got, the man's got enough trouble now, what with the Feds closing in, not that I feel any sympathy for him. But somehow I can't see him behind the killing. And as far as Keller and Corcoran are concerned, neither of them has ever much liked our late senator, although I just can't believe either one would risk his precious position in the community to engineer a murder. As much as I'm against that parkway, it doesn't seem to me that any road is worth killing for.

"Those are just my thoughts, for what they're worth. I'm sure you bright detective types are better at analyzing this kind of situation than one poor ol' country boy who's lucky to have two nickels to rub together."

"I wouldn't necessarily put too much stock in the brains of detective types—other than my boss, of course. Thanks for your time, Mr. Baxter," I said, rising. "By the way," I said, turning back to him, "I did enjoy that quote of yours, the one where you called the senator the biggest traitor in New York State since Benedict Arnold. Very clever. Those big city papers of ours couldn't resist it."

"Why thank you, son. I have to admit I thought that was pretty snappy, too. And I sure enjoyed jawing with you as well. When your boss or the law down there in the big city decides that I'm a killer, just have them come up here. This is where they'll find me—unless I'm out somewhere picketing or marching with those fine young Vassar women from over Poughkeepsie way."

Before leaving Baxter's homey log abode, I told him there was a T-bone steak with his name on it down the road at Nellie's little grocery. That brought the biggest smile that I'd seen on his pleasant, weathered face yet.

Heading the convertible back south, I drove down Route 9, stopping in a roadside diner on the edge of Peekskill for a corned beef sandwich on rye, a glass of milk, and a slice of Dutch apple pie that was as good as I remembered it from a stop I made at the same café years before.

The rest of the trip home was in darkness, and by the time I had garaged the car and rung the buzzer on the stoop, it was almost midnight. Fritz, whom I knew would still be up, unbolted the front door and swung it open. Walking into the empty office, I found a handwritten note on my desk:

A.G.
Please see me at 8:30 a.m.
N.W.

At that hour, Wolfe would still be having breakfast in his bedroom, so apparently the relapse had come to an end almost before it started. As I was absorbing this, Fritz appeared in the doorway. "Archie, I have saved you a plate of the Brazilian lobster salad," he said.

"As I have said many times, you are a prince among men," I told him. "What's been going on here?"

"I think perhaps he is going back to work."

"Really? What makes you say that?"

"Mr. Wolfe answered a telephone call just as I was serving him beer after dinner. The man on the other end was angry, very angry. He was so loud I could hear his voice through the receiver."

"Aha, that sounds like none other than our old friend Inspector Cramer."

He shook his head. "I do not think so, Archie. It was a different voice. This person, whoever he is, will be coming here tomorrow at eleven."

"Well, the day promises to be interesting. Now if you please, bring on that lobster salad. It will give me the strength to cope with the challenges that await."

CHAPTER 11

The next morning at eight thirty, I rapped once on Nero Wolfe's bedroom door, got the word to enter, and stepped in. Wolfe always takes breakfast in his room on a tray Fritz brings up at eight fifteen, sometimes eating in bed, other times on the table by the window. This day, he was at the table, clad, as usual, in canary yellow pajamas that only served to emphasize his volume. He had already polished off his orange juice and a bowl of fresh figs and cream and had started in on the first of two hefty slices of Georgia ham, broiled, of course.

He glowered at me, setting his knife and fork down and dabbing his mouth with a napkin. "You have never met Charles Fentress." It was a statement, not a question.

"No, sir, I haven't. What have I missed?"

"The man is a ninnyhammer. He telephoned here last evening and launched into a tirade about you and, by association, me."

"Really. What have I done to set him off?"

"After Mrs. Fentress met with you yesterday, she went home and told him that you believe he murdered Senator Milbank."

"You may recall that after my meeting with Mona Fentress, I reported to you on our conversation."

114

"I do," Wolfe said as he cut a piece of ham.

"Then you also will recall that I told you she seemed very eager to rile up her husband."

"You quoted her as saying she was going to have fun at his expense over what she called 'this business,' meaning the murder."

"And now it appears that our capricious Mona also is having some fun at my expense, as well. At no time did I suggest to her that I considered her husband a suspect, let alone the prime suspect."

Wolfe scowled. "During our acrimonious conversation, I told him you are not in the habit of making unfounded allegations, but he refused to listen. We talked around each other for several minutes before he demanded that you and I meet with him either at his advertising agency office or his home. I said such was impossible, that we would meet with him here or not at all. He bridled and whined at my ultimatum but finally acquiesced. He is to arrive at eleven."

"I can hardly wait," I said with an exaggerated groan.

"I share your lack of enthusiasm, but perhaps we may learn more about the circumstances leading to Senator Milbank's death from the angry and petulant Mr. Fentress."

"Yeah, maybe. Before I go downstairs, do you want me to report on my activities of yesterday?"

Wolfe nodded and went on attacking his breakfast as I filled him in on my trip north. He offered no comments during my recitation, and when I was finished and was met with more silence, along with the hint of a nod, I went downstairs to my own breakfast, which I always have at a small table in the kitchen.

As I ate and paged through that morning's *Times*, I could feel Fritz's eyes on me. After finishing the grilled ham and corn fritters, I swiveled in my chair and answered his unspoken question. "The man you heard on the phone with Mr. Wolfe last night is named Charles Fentress. He is coming to visit us at eleven. It will not surprise you to learn that this gentleman is unhappy."

The furrows in Fritz's brow deepened. "Do you think that there will be trouble, Archie?"

"Nothing we won't be able to handle. But look on the bright side: Mr. Wolfe's relapse did not last long at all, which means you will be able to do your work without interference."

That didn't totally erase the frown, but at least Fritz allowed himself a small sigh of relief. The man is a compulsive worrier. He worries when Wolfe isn't working for fear we will go broke. He worries when Wolfe *is* working, concerned that he is not getting enough to eat, if you can believe that. And he worries that when I'm out on a case, following Wolfe's orders, something terrible will happen to me on the mean streets of the greater world beyond the brownstone.

After breakfast, I took a cup of coffee into the office and put the orchid germination records in order. As I finished, the phone rang.

"Nero Wolfe's office, Archie Goodwin speaking."

"Hello, Archie, it's Elise."

"Of course. I recognize your mellifluous voice."

She giggled. "Did anyone ever tell you that you've got a way with words?"

"All the time. I try to add a new one to my vocabulary every day. I have been told it adds to my appeal."

"It certainly does, Archie. I'm curious as to how the investigation is going. What can you tell me?"

"Only that we are hard at work."

"Any specifics?"

"Not at the moment. But if there are developments, you will hear from us."

"Is there something that I can do to help, anything at all?"

"I don't think so, but I'll ask Mr. Wolfe and let you know." She wanted to keep talking, but I politely discouraged her, claiming a heavy workload. In truth, I had no workload whatever at the moment, and what I did accomplish the rest of the morning until eleven o'clock wasn't worth a mention.

The whirring of Wolfe's elevator came seconds before the doorbell rang. The figure I saw through the one-way glass panel in the front door could be described as medium height, dark, and cross.

117

Charles Fentress was clad in a superbly tailored three-piece Glen plaid suit, and his blue silk tie probably cost as much as a four-course meal at Rusterman's.

The bell rang a second time, longer, as I swung the door open. "About time," Fentress snapped. "Who are you?"

"Archie Goodwin. Who are you?"

"You know who I am, and unfortunately, I know too much about you. Your man Wolfe is expecting me, and you will be the subject of our conversation," he said, jabbing an index finger at me. Fentress might have been considered handsome, with his square jaw and close-cropped black hair, except for a surly expression, which may well have been an ever-present condition.

I ushered him in, and he followed me down the hall to the office. "Where's Wolfe?" he demanded as I gestured him to the red leather chair. "He will be here shortly," I said, neglecting to add that he invariably preferred to enter only after his guest or guests had arrived and been seated. Wolfe would deny it, even to me, but he possessed a theatrical streak.

Once our angry guest had dropped into the chair, exhaled loudly, and crossed his legs, Wolfe walked in, detoured around his desk, placed a raceme of orchids in a vase, and dipped his head a quarter of an inch, which for him was a greeting. "Good morning, sir. Would you like to have something to drink—coffee perhaps? I am having beer."

"No, thank you," Fentress said, flashing a monogrammed cuff on his custom-made white-on-white shirt. "I did not come here to socialize."

"I do not equate the offer of a beverage with socializing," Wolfe replied evenly. "It should be expected of any good host."

"I am also not here to discuss etiquette," the advertising executive said stiffly. "I will leave that to Emily Post. Let's get right to the point." He turned toward me. "I am prepared to sue this man for slander, and maybe you, too, while I'm at it."

"Bold talk indeed, Mr. Fentress," Wolfe said, raising his eyebrows and leaning forward. "What is the charge?"

"You know damned well. As I told you on the phone yesterday, your man here has accused me of murdering Orson Milbank."

Fritz brought in beer and Wolfe uncapped the first bottle and poured, watching the foam subside. "When and where did this occurrence take place?" he asked before taking a first sip.

"That's what he told my wife when they met for coffee over at Grand Central Station."

Wolfe turned to me. "Is this true, Archie?"

"It is true that I had coffee with Mrs. Fentress. It is also true that we had that coffee at Grand Central. However, it is not true that I told her I believed her husband had killed Orson Milbank."

Back to Fentress. "Do you consider Mrs. Fentress a reliable source?"

Our guest let out a sound best described as a snarl. "That sounds like an insult to Mona."

"Not at all, sir," Wolfe replied calmly. "But because we are discussing the possible commission of an offense, I merely ask a question that a competent lawyer would surely pose to you on a witness stand."

"My wife would hardly lie to me," Fentress huffed, crossing his arms.

"It is good to know you have such an honest and candid relationship," Wolfe said. "Would others agree?"

"What do you mean by that?"

"I thought the meaning of my question was manifest. How is your marriage viewed by others who know one or both of you?"

Fentress took a deep breath. "I hardly see where that is any of your business."

"You would have a most difficult time in a courtroom, sir," Wolfe said, dabbing his lips with a napkin. "If I were an attorney representing Mr. Goodwin, I believe I would have no problem finding individuals who had witnessed the two of you quarreling in public."

"I might have expected these sorts of dirty tricks out of a private eye," Fentress said with a sneer.

"Dirty tricks? Hardly, sir," Wolfe said. "I am merely showing you how one defends oneself against what might be a baseless charge. I urge you to ask your wife once again to repeat exactly what Mr. Goodwin said to her about you and Senator Milbank."

"And what if she repeats what she had told me before? Then I will file a suit for slander."

"I do not presume to speak for Mr. Goodwin, but it seems likely that he will file a countersuit for defamation. Archie?"

"I've got a lawyer all lined up," I said, "and he's a good one. He's eager to take me on as a client. I believe you know him."

"Yes, I do, and he is among the very best in the city, if not the entire nation," Wolfe said, leaning back in his desk chair and interlacing his fingers over his middle mound. "There you are, sir—a standoff. What is your decision?"

Fentress studied his pricey wristwatch and frowned. "I will talk to Mona again," he said in a voice just above a whisper.

"A sound course of action," Wolfe said. "But while we are on the subject of Orson Milbank, I gather you did not like him."

"I don't recall ever having said that."

"But in public quarrels with your wife on more than one occasion, you were heard loudly berating the senator because of the long hours that you claimed he made her work."

Fentress nodded. "I won't deny that I didn't like the man, but just for the sake of argument, let's

121

say I killed him, or had him killed. What in God's name would be my motive?"

"Jealousy?" I put in.

"Because he and Mona spent so much time together? Oh, don't worry," he snapped, holding up a palm. "I've heard the rumors about them, and maybe they are true. But then, we're all men of the world in this room, right?" He mood changed suddenly, and he gave us a smile similar to those he probably bestowed upon clients of his agency over cocktails when he was about to tell an off-color joke. "Here's the thing. Mona is free to do what she wants, and so am I, if you get my drift."

I could tell Wolfe was working to hide his disgust with the man, and he did a good job of it. "Let us stipulate, sir, that any animus you might have had toward the late senator involved his having your wife work long hours—nothing more. Having established that, can you suggest anyone who would want Mr. Milbank dead?"

"The obvious choice, of course, is that hoodlum Bacelli. Hell, I read the papers and listen to the news on the air, so I know all about how angry he got when Milbank backed off of his original route for that parkway heading up north. On top of that, Mona told me that Bacelli phoned Milbank several times in a rage. She answered the phone once when he called the office, and she had to listen to a rant that turned the air blue."

"Worthy of note," Wolfe said. "Anyone else you would care to nominate?"

"I'm really the wrong person to answer that, since I had very little to do with Milbank and his work. Based on Mona's comments to me, I'd say Bacelli would easily be at the top of the list. A couple of others who didn't like the senator are Jonah Keller, that real estate guy up north, and a man named Corcoran, I forget his first name, who runs some sort of chamber of commerce, also north of here. But I'm probably not telling you anything you don't already know."

"It is always helpful to get another person's perspective," Wolfe remarked.

Fentress stroked his chiseled chin. "I'm curious about who hired you," he said, returning to his angry mode and switching his attention to me. "Mona told me you wouldn't say who the client was. Is it her?"

"I am afraid I cannot answer that," Wolfe responded.

"Well, I won't take any more of your time," Fentress said, getting to his feet. He was clearly miffed again, and neither Wolfe nor I was the least bit concerned.

CHAPTER 12

After escorting Charles Fentress down the hall to the front door and getting not so much as a thank-you or even a nod for my effort, I returned to the office, where Wolfe had his nose in one of his three current books, *Crusade in Europe* by Dwight Eisenhower. "Well, what do you think of today's guest?" I asked. "Would you still term him a ninnyhammer?"

Wolfe slipped his gold bookmark into the volume and closed it. "My initial opinion remains unchanged," he said. "No, let me amend that: It is even lower than previously."

"Yeah, he sure hasn't taken the time to read Mr. Carnegie's *How to Win Friends and Influence People*, has he? I find it hard to believe he can really turn on the charm when he's wining and dining his agency's clients at one of the town's most expensive eateries."

Wolfe made a face. "From what the man indicated, he honors his wedding vows no more than his wife does hers. I hesitate to give you this assignment, given its distasteful nature, but can you ask Mr. Cohen if he or one of his army of minions can determine the identity of Mr. Fentress's paramour?"

"Sure, although there may be more than one."

That drew another grimace. We were now getting into perilous territory. As I mentioned earlier, Wolfe would not take divorce cases or investigations involving infidelity, and we were now skirting that taboo area, if not downright stepping across the line.

Just before we went into the dining room for lunch, I phoned Lon Cohen. "Geez, Archie, that's not the kind of question I usually get from the esteemed office of one Nero Wolfe."

"I know, and it feels strange asking it. But as somebody, don't ask me who, once said, 'drastic times call for drastic measures.'"

"Well, this newspaper invests enough—probably too much if you want my opinion—in gossip columnists, so I should be able to come up with something for you and your boss to chew on, assuming these scandal mongers of ours are doing their job. Does this have to do with Madison Avenue's Charles Fentress maybe being a murder suspect? Now that would be one hell of a story! I can see the headline already."

"Beats me, Lon. I doubt it very much, but then, I'm not privy to the workings of the brain of Nero Wolfe."

"Is anyone? Anyway, I'll see what I can find out. Just try to remember who your friends are."

"How can I not? You remind me every day," I shot back. "I eagerly await the results of your fact-finding expedition."

Lunch and the afternoon that followed were uneventful—until Wolfe came down from his afternoon session in the plant rooms. He had just gotten his seventh of a ton settled behind the desk when the doorbell rang. I went down the hall and saw a familiar blocky figure through the glass.

"Cramer," I said, returning to the office. "After what's happened today, we're going to have to dig a moat around the brownstone, stock it with alligators, and build a drawbridge to keep undesirables away. Well, do I let him in?"

"Confound it, yes," Wolfe grumped. I went back to the front door and swung it open, admitting Inspector Lionel T. Cramer, head of the New York Police Department's Homicide Squad. "How nice of you to drop in," I told him as he bulled by me and charged down the hall under a full head of steam like a locomotive running behind schedule.

By the time I got to the office, Cramer had planted himself in the red leather chair at one end of Wolfe's desk and had pulled out a cigar, which he jammed into his mouth, unlit as usual.

"By God, you have done it again, you and Goodwin," he growled by way of opening the conversation.

Wolfe looked up from his book, expressionless. "I am about to have a beer. Would you like something?"

"I would not! Don't change the subject."

"I am unaware that a subject has been introduced, sir."

"Oh, stop playing dumb, Wolfe; it doesn't become you, of all people. You know damned well what brought me here. Why is it that every time there's a high-profile murder case in this town, you seem to be right there, Nero on the spot, ready to rake in a fat fee."

Wolfe closed his book and placed it on the desk blotter. He drew in air, exhaling slowly. "Sir, you have barged in here with no advance notice, which I concede is not unusual behavior for you, although it tends to inconvenience me. Now that I have been inconvenienced, you have my attention, at least for the moment. However, you remain here at my forbearance, and if you abuse your privileges as a guest, you will be asked to leave."

"I will be damned. That pretty little speech sounded almost rehearsed," Cramer said, leaning forward in the chair and putting his hat on the floor. "Were you expecting me?"

"I was not, sir," Wolfe said, "although I must admit I rarely am surprised by your visits."

"And you know that the reason for this visit is the shooting of Senator Orson Milbank."

"I do now, because you just told me," Wolfe said as Fritz entered with beer.

"Still being cute, eh? All right, try this one on

for size: A complaint came in to the department and got sent up the line to me because it may have some connection to the Milbank homicide. It seems that a Westchester County resident of some note named Jonah Keller—sound familiar?—got into a wrestling match in his office in White Plains with a man who identified himself as Archie Goodwin. This Goodwin, so Mr. Keller says, had come up to question him about Milbank's death. Now what am I to make of this event?" the inspector posed, turning to me. Wolfe also turned my way, dipping his chin.

"Let the record show that the aforesaid Mr. Keller attacked me and I was defending myself, although I would hardly describe our brief little set-to as a wrestling match. It lasted barely thirty seconds. If you are interested in the outcome, I won. It was no contest."

"More cuteness, huh? And just what might you have said that spurred Keller to violence?"

"Enough of this," Wolfe snapped. "Inspector, to move this discussion along, Mr. Goodwin and I stipulate that he indeed was in Jonah Keller's office and that a contretemps ensued."

"Contretemps?" Cramer took the cigar out of his mouth, staring at it as if he were surprised. "All right, if that's what you choose to call it. Now on to the real business here. Who is your client?"

"Come now, sir," Wolfe said. "You know me better than to ask that question."

"I know you better than to expect any cooperation at any time."

"We both are aware that clearly is not true, sir. In the past, we have shared a great deal of information with each other."

"Yeah, well, what have you got to share with me right now?"

Wolfe flipped a palm. "So far, nothing. We are early in our investigation. What can you tell us?"

Cramer frowned. "That is just how these conversations always seem to turn out. Most of what you call 'sharing' goes down a one-way street. I unload what I've got and you keep your lip zipped."

"On the other hand," Wolfe said, "I think you will agree that on a number of occasions, I have been of some help to you in identifying individuals who later were incarcerated or—"

"Or terminated," Cramer said with a dry laugh. "Okay, okay, I will concede you that point. So you want to know where we are with the Milbank business."

"That might be helpful," Wolfe murmured.

"Probably not so helpful," the inspector said, "because we aren't much of anywhere. As you can learn from any newspaper these days, the fatal shot came from the left-field upper-deck stands at the Polo Grounds, so I assume you know that much. We found a shell casing between two seats up in those stands, .30 caliber."

"Just one casing?" Wolfe asked.

"Yeah, the shooter needed only a single shot, which, as you know, hit Milbank in the temple," Cramer said, "although any decent marksman should be able to nail a target from less than three hundred feet away. After all, the Polo Grounds has that ridiculously short left-field fence, so the seats in those outfield grandstands, even the ones in the upper deck, are fairly close to where Milbank's party was sitting near home plate. Our ballistics boys say the chances are good, but not a sure thing, that the shot came from a semi-automatic .30 caliber M1 Garand rifle because there are so many of them around. They were the standard service rifles for our soldiers and marines during the war. As you know, my son was stationed with the air corps in Australia, so he didn't have need of a rifle. But, Goodwin, you were in the army; you may have fired one."

"I did, during a stint in officer training. It is a fine weapon, no question about it. In fact, no less than the late General George Patton was quoted as calling it 'the greatest battle implement ever devised.' "

"If Patton himself said that, it's good enough for me," Cramer stated. "Anyway, at the moment, we're scrambling, and as you know, the whole department is feeling the heat, all the way up the line to the commissioner—and hell, to the mayor as well."

"What is the prevailing feeling about Mr. Bacelli as a possible suspect?" Wolfe asked.

Cramer gave a shrug. "Part of me would like it to be him—that's to stay in this room, you understand. I don't know, though. I realize he had said some pretty rough things about Milbank when the senator eased up his stance on that road, but whether he's the one behind the shooting is another matter altogether. Right now, it seems like he has got plenty of problems with the Feds without risking trouble over the assassination of an elected official."

Wolfe finished his first bottle of beer and opened the second. "Is it not true, however, Inspector, that the man has been able over a long period to orchestrate killings with impunity?"

Cramer nodded, pursing his lips. "I'm sorry to say there's no question about it, and that's a point in the thug's favor as a suspect. Our men have talked to him, and you won't be surprised to learn that he has an alibi for the afternoon of the shooting, which means nothing, since he has probably never pulled a trigger himself, at least not since his earliest days as a wheelman for rum-runners with the Mob, back during Prohibition."

"May I ask who else you have questioned?"

"Yeah, you can, but I expect something in return," Cramer said. "I've changed my mind about a drink. I'll have a beer."

Wolfe's face registered surprise. "I thought you preferred bourbon?"

"I usually do, but I'm in a beer mood. Yours looks good, and I'm thirsty."

"I'm on the case," I said, heading for the kitchen. When I got back with an opened bottle and a chilled pilsner glass, Cramer was in mid-sentence. ". . . so one of my men spent almost an hour up in White Plains talking to Jonah Keller, who was offended that we would even dare to question him about his relationship to Milbank, let alone suspect him of murder. He got really riled, so it's not surprising that he mixed it up with Goodwin a few days later. Paranoia had set in."

"Who else have you talked to?"

Cramer took a swig of beer and set his glass on the small table next to him. "There's another guy up that way named Ray Corcoran, who like Keller had no use for the senator. He heads up a business group and is a somewhat smoother customer than Keller. You may have heard of him."

Wolfe looked at me and again dipped his head a fraction of an inch. "We have more than heard of him, Inspector," I said, picking up on Wolfe's cue. "I have talked to him in his office up north, and I agree that he is a smoother number than Jonah the Jackass—maybe a little too smooth for my taste."

132

"Archie also visited a gentleman who heads up that antigrowth organization, Citizens Looking to Enjoy Arboreal Nature," Wolfe volunteered.

"Oh yeah," Cramer said. "We've heard of that bunch, although I didn't bother to have anybody talk to their honcho. They seem okay, and from what I know, he's harmless, if a little on the strange side."

"I would say that squares with my impression of Howell Baxter," I said, "although I found him to be quite pleasant, an engaging character who loves trees and parks and doesn't have much use for wide new roads, no matter what route they take. As I'm sure you know, his small group generally liked Milbank, at least until recently, when the senator backed off from his total opposition to the parkway, and then they—or at least Baxter—called him a traitor. Baxter claims he's a pacifist, and for all that I know he is. Most of the people from CLEAN, as they call themselves, are volunteers, including a bunch of coeds from Vassar."

Cramer drank more beer, then leaned back and pressed his palms to his eyes. "The heat is on us like I've never seen it before, never," he groaned. "When the newspapers aren't hammering on the department, the so-called better-government groups are. You probably read that there have been calls for the commissioner's scalp, and if Humbert gets the boot, I'll probably get tossed out

133
North Central Kansas Libraries

the door and find myself out on the sidewalk beside him."

"Surely you do not believe your job is in jeopardy," Wolfe said, sounding genuinely surprised.

"Don't be too sure of that. Over the years, I've survived the firing squad during some rough times, but as I just told you, this is the worst, and by far. In a way, I suppose I'd feel some relief getting out of the pressure cooker. I haven't had a decent vacation in years. My wife's been after me to spend a couple of weeks in Florida this winter, and I can't remember the last time I've been fishing for anything more than a long weekend."

"You know that you'd go buggy after even a few days away from the office," I told him.

"Well, if the newspaper editorial writers and the holier-than-thou reformers get their way, maybe I'll have a chance to find out before too long," Cramer said, slapping his battered fedora on his head and rising to leave. "Thanks for the beer," he told Wolfe. "If you learn anything you care to share, let me know."

"That's the quietest exit he's made in years," I said when I got back to the office after seeing him out. "He came in like a lion but left like a lamb. He's just not the same old grouch we have come to know. It's sad, really."

"Mr. Cramer is being besieged on several

fronts," Wolfe remarked. "Nothing stirs mass emotions like the killing of a public figure. The inspector marched in angry because it has become a habit for him to behave that way in this house. It is as if he were an actor typecast in a role. And in this case, his behavior also was to cover his embarrassment at conceding that he is at an impasse."

I nodded. "You certainly were cooperative with him, offering up everything that we've got so far."

Wolfe raised his shoulders and let them drop. "And why not? What we have is hardly of significance, and perhaps at some point Mr. Cramer will reciprocate."

"If he is still around to reciprocate, that is."

"Archie, we both are well aware the inspector is extremely honest and extremely good at his job, despite some inadequacies, examples of which we have seen over the years. I cannot believe the police department and the City of New York would be so imbecilic as to dispense with his services. They would be hard-pressed to find a suitable replacement."

"I hope you're right. It may sound strange for me to say this, but I would miss his visits."

Wolfe chose not to respond, returning to his book.

CHAPTER 13

The next morning, I got off to a late start, having danced with Lily at the Flamingo Club until well past midnight. When I finally settled in at my desk following breakfast, it was after ten, and I had just begun to type Wolfe's correspondence when the phone rang.

"Good morning, Archie," Lon Cohen said. "I certainly hope I'm not interrupting anything important."

"At the moment, I can think of nothing more important than a call from you. What news do you bring from the world of printing presses and deadlines and violent deaths?"

"A pair of items, of varying importance. First, a certain woman of your acquaintance is holding a press conference at noon today up in White Plains that I believe you will find interesting."

"Really? By all means, tell me more."

"Let me read you the key portion of a press release that got delivered to our office—and I assume to the wire services, all the other local papers, and radio and television stations—this morning: " 'It is with a sense of both humility and duty that I today announce my candidacy for the state senate seat that had been occupied so nobly and for so long by the martyred Orson D.

Milbank. Having worked closely with this fine public servant for many years, I firmly and earnestly believe that I am uniquely qualified to continue his tireless and selfless work for the betterment of his many thousands of constituents.

" 'There has been no finer champion of the public interest in this state than Senator Milbank, whose life was so tragically cut short by an assassin's bullet. As for my candidacy, I am proud to say that the Empire State has pioneered in electing women to public office, having had females in the New York legislature since 1919. These women have been an inspiration to me, as has Margaret Chase Smith of Maine, who serves with courage and integrity in the United States Senate.' That's the gist of it, Archie, although it goes on, with Mrs. Fentress heaping further praise upon the martyred senator," Lon said. "Do you want to hear more? There's another full page."

"No, that will hold me for the present. What does your political editor up in Albany think of all this?"

"He figures the comely Mrs. Fentress is a cinch to get the party's nod and has a pretty fair chance of winning in the fall. The guy who would have gone up against Milbank—and will surely run against her—is competent but hardly exciting. What she has got going for her is the sympathy vote and the obvious fact that she's a looker. You can't overestimate that factor."

"I suppose not. You newspaper types are pushovers for glamour. I'll be damned, Mona Fentress a senator."

"Not yet, Archie, but she's off to what seems like a good start," Lon said. "Imagine the publicity she will get from her announcement today. Everybody, including even the *Times*, will play this on page one, and most of the papers— including us—will run a multi-column photo of the lady. And then, of course, there are the television stations, our relatively new competition, which seem to go even further overboard than we do over any story that involves a pretty face."

"She gave out no clue about this when I had coffee with her a couple of days ago. I wonder whose idea it was."

"Our Albany man thinks it originated with her and her alone. He says the lady is ambitious— very ambitious. He also pointed out that one drawback to her candidacy is that she may well be seen as a blatant opportunist, and I have to agree with him on that."

"You said you had two items of importance, although you'll have to go some to top that one."

"Staying on the subject of the Fentress family, you wanted to know if the advertising man has a . . . special friend," Lon said. "The answer is yes, according to those on the *Gazette* staff who earn their keep by ferreting out this type of information. The woman in question is Caroline

Jackson Willis, described to me as a twice-divorced socialite. 'Socialite' is a word that can carry many meanings, as you probably are aware, Archie."

"You mean such as 'idle rich' or 'gold digger' or on a more positive note, 'patroness of the arts'?"

"You get the idea. Giving the lady the benefit of the doubt, Mrs. Willis probably best fits into your last category, what with her being on all sorts of museum boards and such, although she could fit into the other two slots as well, seeing as how both her husbands were very well fixed. Anyway, rumors have it that she and Fentress have been together on occasion, mostly at discreet private parties in places like Park Avenue duplexes, rubbing shoulders with other members of the Social Register."

I made a mental note to ask Lily about Mrs. Willis. "You're filled with interesting information today, Mr. Newspaperman."

"You're welcome. Now does all of this entitle me to get the name of your client?"

" 'Fraid you'll just have to wait on that—at least until I get the green light from Mr. Wolfe."

A prolonged sigh came from the other end. "And after all that I've done for the two of you."

"Believe me, it is much appreciated. But as you told Mr. Wolfe yourself at dinner, you've gotten as good as you've given in our dealings over the years." Lon conceded the point, and we signed off just as Wolfe entered the office, fresh from his morning visit with the orchids.

While he got settled and rang for beer, I reported on Lon's discoveries. He listened, but seemed distracted. "The *Gazette*," he pronounced.

"Yes, the *Gazette*, as in Lon Cohen. Now what do you think about what he just told me on the tele—"

"The *Gazette*, four days ago, Archie. I admit to being guilty of opacity. The death notices, third column, middle of the page, surname Thompson. Get it."

As a matter of course, we keep copies of the *Times* and the *Gazette* for three weeks. I went to the shelf and pulled out the requested edition, turning to the page with the death notices and found the item.

THOMPSON, RICHARD, 29—A heroic marine from Queens who served valiantly in World War II. He was a superb rifleman, earning the Marine Rifle Sharpshooting Badge, the Bronze Star, the Navy and Marine Corps Medal, and the Purple Heart. Fighting on Okinawa, he was credited with killing nineteen Japanese. He is deeply mourned by his sister, Marguerite Hackman of Queens. Services have been held.

After reading it over twice, I turned to Wolfe. "Seems like a long shot, pardon the pun," I said, handing the page to him.

"Perhaps, but here we have: one, a skilled marksman dead; two, an apparently premature death; and three, a death that took place shortly after the killing of Mr. Milbank. As you know, I always have been suspicious of coincidences. Call Mr. Cohen and find out if his newspaper has further information on this marine and the circumstances of his demise."

"Our last conversation ended with him wanting some quid pro quo, specifically the identity of our client. Now he'll really be after me to cough it up."

Wolfe drew in air and exhaled. "Very well. Give him what he wants with the stipulation that her name not be released without my permission. He will honor that."

I agreed with him and dialed Lon. "You again? Look, I just gave you everything I had. My cupboard is empty, honest it is."

I told him about the Thompson item, which he quickly located. "I'll be damned, I always go through the paid death notices that come in— chalk it up to my morbid curiosity," Lon said. "But this guy didn't register with me, although I have to say that even rereading it now, this seems like it's a reach."

"Exactly what I told Wolfe. But he wants to find

out more about Thompson and the cause of death. You're a seasoned newshound. This is the kind of thing you can find out a lot easier than Wolfe or me."

"You're a fine one to be doling out cheap flattery, Archie. Give me one reason why I should do this for you when you won't even tell me who your client is." Then I told him.

"I'll be a monkey's uncle, although I'm really not surprised. I suspected it was the bereaved widow."

"So now you know, but nobody else does. Let's keep it that way."

"Aye, aye, sir. I will get back to you when I find out something about one Richard Thompson."

CHAPTER 14

After I hung up, the doorbell rang. I walked down the hall to the front door and peeked through the one-way glass, getting a surprise. "What I suggested the other day about building a moat around this place is really worth considering," I told Wolfe back in the office, silently mouthing a name.

"Egad," he said, eyes wide. "Well, bring him in."

I opened the door, keeping the chain on. "I have come here to see Nero Wolfe," the older and better dressed of two men on the stoop said. "I am—"

"I know who you are. And just who is he?" I demanded, gesturing to the other one.

"He goes everywhere with me."

"Not in here, he doesn't. If you want to see Nero Wolfe, you are free to enter—and alone. Otherwise, it's no soap. That's the way things are around here, period. Take it or leave it."

After a long pause punctuated with a mutter, the older man shrugged. "Go back to the car, Victor," he said calmly. I waited until Victor had descended the steps and was getting into a black Lincoln sedan idling at the curb before I opened the door to our guest.

I took his homburg from him and hung it on the

rack near the door. He then followed me down the hall to the office, where I steered him to the red leather chair. "Mr. Wolfe," he said with a dip of the head as he sat.

"Mr. Bacelli," Wolfe acknowledged.

"You recognize me?" the Mob kingpin said with a tight smile, running a hand over his full and well-tended head of silver-gray hair.

"You jest. Certainly I do. Your photograph has been in the New York newspapers so often over the years that I am confident eighty percent of the residents of this city would recognize you if they passed you on the street."

That brought a dry laugh. "You're right, yes, you are. At least when I walk out of a courtroom and the press photographers start snapping their damned pictures, I don't put a hat or copy of the *Herald Tribune* over my face like some of my, shall we say . . . colleagues," he said, stroking a mustache that was suspiciously darker than the hair on his dome. "I don't hide from anybody, never have, never will."

Wolfe considered his visitor though narrowed eyes. "Would you like something to drink? I am about to have beer."

"Nothing, thanks," Franco Bacelli said, holding up a hand adorned by a gold ring studded with small diamonds. "Ulcers have put an end to my drinking days, I'm sad to say."

"A pity. What brings you here?"

"Look, Mr. Wolfe, I won't beat around the bush; it's not my style. You are investigating Milbank's murder—don't ask me how I know. I have come here to offer my help."

"Indeed?" Wolfe's face registered surprise.

"I know that to some people, I am an obvious suspect in the killing of Milbank, given things I've said to the senator and about him, especially after he weaseled out of his total opposition to that damned parkway," Bacelli said. "But I have got lots bigger problems right now than having a new road ruin the peace and quiet of my neighborhood up north."

"Your problems have been well chronicled," Wolfe observed as Fritz entered with his beer.

Another sour laugh from the mobster. "They sure as Hades have. A lot of people are out to get me, and I am damned if I'm going to make things any easier for them by getting tagged with this Polo Grounds shooting. Hell, I had absolutely nothing to do with it. Nothing." As I studied Bacelli from my desk, I could not decide whether his chiseled profile was better suited to a Roman coin or a WANTED poster.

"You said you came here to offer help," Wolfe said. "How do you propose to do that?"

"I've got lots of sources, lots of ways to find out exactly how Milbank got rubbed out," Bacelli said, studying his cufflink. "I could get started today, just like that," he went on, snapping his fingers. "It wouldn't cost you a cent, not a penny."

"It might well cost me a great deal more than money," Wolfe commented. "I thank you for your offer, but I must decline."

"Too proud to take my help, is that it?" Bacelli said.

"I assure you pride has absolutely nothing to do with my decision, sir," Wolfe snapped. "I believe I can reach my goals through far different channels than I suspect you are likely to utilize."

Bacelli showed a set of pearly whites in what seemed to be a cross between a smile and a sneer. "Pretty damned sure of yourself, aren't you?"

"I prefer the word confident. My methods have worked reasonably well through the years."

"Is that so? Well, suit yourself, Mr. Nero Wolfe," Bacelli said with a tilt of his chin. "But I am going to find out who took care of the senator anyway, and I'll do it before you do, I guarantee that. That will screw you out of your fee. Whatever else happens to me, they are not going to pin the killing of a senator on this tough old Sicilian, I guarantee that."

Bacelli rose, brushed an imaginary hair from the sleeve of his navy blue pinstriped silk suit, and executed a snappy about-face, striding out of the office. I accompanied him down the hall to the front door and was met with the same silent treatment I had gotten from Charles Fentress and

Cramer when they left the brownstone. At this rate, I could get a complex.

"Well, just what do you make of that?" I asked Wolfe back in the office.

"Incredible," he said after drinking beer and eyeing the unopened book on his desk blotter. "Whatever made him think that I would go along with—oh, enough of this. I can only imagine how the man would set about extracting information."

"Yeah, and it sounds as if he's going to push ahead without you. As I asked at the moment when we were so rudely interrupted by Mr. Bacelli the Sicilian, what are my instructions?"

Wolfe drew in air and exhaled slowly. "I would like to talk to the others on Senator Milbank's staff. In addition to Mrs. Fentress, I believe there were three of them in the group at the baseball game."

"Yes, Keith Musgrove, who did polling for Milbank; Todd Armstrong, an intern on the senator's staff who had recently graduated from NYU; and Ross Davies, the campaign manager and strategist."

"See if you can get them all here tonight at eight thirty."

"So you're not tired of having people storm our battlements yet?" Wolfe opened his book without answering me.

CHAPTER 15

I dialed Mona Fentress to get phone numbers of the trio Wolfe wanted to see. "Oh . . . hello, Archie, I wasn't expecting to hear from you today," she said.

"Oh, I'm always full of surprises, but then, so are you it would seem, including putting words in my mouth just for the sport of seeing your husband get himself all riled up. He put on quite a performance in front of Mr. Wolfe and me. And while we are on the subject of surprises, exactly when did you decide to run for Milbank's senate seat?"

"I honestly had not made up my mind yet when I saw you, and that's the truth. But one question had been going through my mind for days: Who would Orson want to succeed him? I finally came to the realization that it would be me. I hope that does not sound arrogant."

"Not particularly. People running for office must be sure of themselves and project self-confidence. What does your husband think about your decision?"

"I didn't ask him, Archie, and honestly, at this point I don't care. But in the past, he has said more than once that he doesn't feel women have the temperament to be in politics and government.

He's out in California on business right now, trying to help his agency land a new client, some winery I think, so he's in for a surprise when he gets back."

"I'll say. It sounds like he won't be part of your campaign team, huh? Sorry—that was uncalled for."

"That's all right, Archie," she said with a laugh. "I could use a little humor these days."

"Between us, and not for publication, what do you think your chances are in the fall?"

"Keith Musgrove—he was Orson's pollster and now he's going to work for me—thinks we are in pretty good shape. He'll know more when he starts doing some canvassing in the coming weeks."

"Speaking of Mr. Musgrove, I'd like to get his phone number along with those of Ross Davies and Todd Armstrong."

"Really? Whatever for?"

"Beats me. Nero Wolfe barks orders, and I carry them out. Long ago, I learned my role in this operation."

"Well . . . of course, I've got them here," Mona said. "Please hold the line."

She came on less than a minute later and read me the numbers, although she didn't sound particularly happy about it. "Is there anything I should know?" she asked.

"Not that I am aware of. Bear in mind that Mr.

Wolfe is a genius, and he works in strange and wondrous ways, most of which are totally beyond my comprehension. Thanks for those numbers, and best of luck. I would be proud to one day address you as Madam Senator." Mona Fentress would have liked to pump me further, but I closed the conversation.

I reached all three men on my first try, and none sounded overjoyed to get an invitation to the brownstone. Both Keith Musgrove and Todd Armstrong complained that they had told the police everything they remembered about that afternoon at the Polo Grounds, and Musgrove demanded to know who had hired us. I side-stepped his question and wore down his resistance by pointing out that Nero Wolfe was the best hope for finding Milbank's killer, especially given the ineffectiveness of the police so far.

Young Mr. Armstrong was easier to persuade since I pointed out that Musgrove already had agreed to come to West Thirty-Fifth Street. Ross Davies offered the least resistance, conceding that he had read about Wolfe for many years and claimed to be intrigued by the possibility of meeting him.

The three arrived together precisely at eight thirty. They formed quite a contrast. Musgrove, easily the eldest, was also the shortest, no more than five foot five, and the one most likely to stand out in a crowd. He sported horn-rimmed glasses with lenses as thick as the bottoms of cola bottles, which magnified his blinking eyes, giving him a permanently deranged appearance. He combed his once-dark hair—what was left of it—all the way across his head in a futile attempt to camouflage his near baldness. Todd Armstrong was a college graduate but looked nearer to eighteen, his baby face accented by innocent blue eyes and center-parted blond hair. Ross Davies, about halfway between the others in age—say mid- or late-thirties—was a healthy-looking specimen with an intelligent expression and a posture worthy of a military officer, which I was to learn he had been.

"Gentlemen, please step right in," I told them, "and thank you all for coming. Mr. Wolfe would like to see you separately. Who would like to go first?"

"Why do we need to see him separately?" Davies demanded. "This could take all night."

"No, sir, I assure you it will not. Mr. Wolfe is always direct and to the point. In all my years here, I have never known him to waste anyone's time. Now, if one of you volunteers to see him first, the others can wait in the front room, where there will be refreshments and reading material."

"Oh, all right, I'll go first, why not?" Davies said. He seemed to be the take-charge guy of the three. I ushered the others into the front room, closing the door behind them, then walked Davies down the hall to the office. After he got seated in the red leather chair, Wolfe entered the room and I made the introductions. I then went to the kitchen, giving Fritz the heads-up that two of our guests in the front room might like a drink, alcoholic or otherwise.

Back in the office, Davies was talking. "I assumed you would have wanted to see all of us together," he told Wolfe amiably.

"I prefer this approach, sir, because I like to hear individual impressions of what happened at the baseball stadium, not those impressions influenced by what someone else has just described. Before we start, would you like something to drink? As you see, I am having beer." Davies requested scotch and water, which I mixed at the wheeled cart against one wall.

"Where do you want to start?" Davies asked after taking a sip of the scotch and nodding his approval.

"At the moment you entered the Polo Grounds, sir," Wolfe said. "I realize you have related these events to the police in detail, probably more than once, but please humor me."

"Fair enough. As I'm sure you have become aware, Orson was a big fan and a big booster of the American flag. That morning, he gave the rest of us small flags, and we walked down to our front-row seats waving them. Even though I love our flag and have fought for it, I felt a little foolish, as

I'm sure several of the others did, but . . ." He turned his palms up in a gesture of helplessness. "I respect the chain of command, and if that is what Orson wanted, then I was on board. I was an army captain during the war, so I am used to both giving orders and taking them.

"Back to the game," Davies continued, squaring his shoulders. "The first few innings were uneventful. There was no scoring, and little if anything to root about, as again I am sure you are aware. Because both teams are from New York City, Orson urged us to be rigidly impartial and cheer equally for each of them. So when that home run got hit in the fourth, we all jumped to our feet waving our flags and yelling, and then, well . . . Orson keeled over and Mona started screaming. None of us—and that includes Mona—realized immediately what had just happened. We could not possibly have heard a distant shot over all of that crowd noise."

"Were you sitting next to the senator?" Wolfe asked.

"No, I was two seats to his right, with Mona between us. Everything occurred so quickly. It must have been just moments before Orson got shot that Mona fell against me. I later learned that the heel of her shoe had snapped off. She said afterward that Orson had leaned over to grab her to stop her fall, and at that moment he was hit."

Wolfe drew in air and exhaled. "Is it correct

that you were the senator's second-in-command?"

"My titles—campaign manager and strategist—might indeed have led one to believe that," Davies said in a sour tone. "But in reality, Mona was the real number two in the operation. She had Orson's ear on almost everything to do with his office and his campaigns. The power behind the throne, you might say."

"Were you surprised when she announced her candidacy for the senator's seat?" Wolfe asked.

"Not really. And I am not surprised that she never said anything to me about it, not one word, either. I had to read about it in the papers like almost everyone else. Mona has always been extremely ambitious. Oh, she makes an attempt to hide it behind a veneer of modesty and self-effacement, but for anyone who's been around her for very long, it's clear that ambition bubbles up just below the surface. It's not hard to detect if one is around her for very long. I liken her to a caged animal just waiting to be turned loose."

"I assume Mrs. Fentress has not asked you to be a part of her campaign."

"You assume correctly, Mr. Wolfe," Davies said, tight-lipped. "Although I've heard via the grapevine that she's hired Musgrove to do her polling. He hasn't said anything to me, however, even though we were in a taxi together for twenty minutes coming over here. I have not asked him about it, nor am I about to."

"Has there been what one would describe as animus between you and Mrs. Fentress?" Wolfe posed.

"I find animus to be far too strong a word, Mr. Wolfe. Rather, I would describe our relationship as being marked by a certain amount of mutual distrust, although most of the distrust is on my side. Mona has little if any reason to distrust me."

"How would you describe Mrs. Fentress's relationship to the senator?"

Davies looked down at his glass for several seconds before responding. "Any answer I give you would be pure speculation, I'm afraid."

"This is a confidential conversation, sir," Wolfe said, "with Mr. Goodwin every bit as closed-mouthed as am I. Much of what has been said in this room over the years has been speculation. On many occasions, speculation voiced here has led to the solution of a problem."

Davies frowned, seeming to be at odds with himself. "There was some talk," he finally said after finishing his drink, "that they were more than just working colleagues."

"Did you see evidence of that, sir?"

"What I would term circumstantial evidence only. They often dined together, danced in public places, and seemed fixated upon each other, beyond what any professional collaboration called for. All that, of course, led to gossip—gossip, by the way, that I scrupulously avoided being a party to or passing along."

"Do you have a sense of how their spouses felt about this situation?"

Davies snorted. "It was pretty clear how Charles Fentress felt. More than once, he made a scene, complaining loudly that Orson was working his wife too hard. At least that was what he claimed his beef was about. As to Mrs. Milbank—or Miss DuVal, if you prefer—I have no idea what she thought about her husband's relationship to Mona. I didn't see her often at fund-raisers, speeches, or other political events. She preferred to stay out of the limelight most of the time."

"She is an attractive woman," Wolfe said. "Would not she have been an asset to her husband by being seen with him more often in public?"

"You raise a very good point. After all, she had been a film actress of sorts, for heaven's sake, so she was used to playing roles. And being the wife of an officeholder certainly entails playing a role—an extremely important one. I can think of several wives who have won—and lost—elections for their spouses. I don't mean to say Elise was invisible, but she did not attend as many events as you might expect of a senator's wife, particularly those events that were held up in Albany. I have heard that she didn't care for that town, pre-ferring the bright lights and the social whirl of

Manhattan. Pretty hard for our humble old state capital to compete with that."

"Another question, Mr. Davies: Do you have any thoughts as to who might have wanted the senator dead?"

I had refilled Davies's scotch, and he took a sip before answering. "The obvious answer would seem to be Franco Bacelli, wouldn't it?" he said. "Especially given their recent history. But I don't buy that."

"Why not, sir?"

A shrug. "Somehow, I simply cannot see the mobster orchestrating a killing that had the potential for giving him nothing but headaches. He's got enough of those from Uncle Sam right now, as has been well reported in the newspapers. And, of course, I am all too aware of the business interests in his district that were pushing for that Northern Parkway. Some of them, notably Jonah Keller and Ray Corcoran, were mad as hell at Orson. But to shoot someone over a road?" Davies folded his arms across his chest and shook his head. "Sorry, Mr. Wolfe, but to me that makes absolutely no sense. My theory, for what it's worth, is that among the thousands of people in his district, there was some mentally deranged individual who felt, God only knows why, that Orson had done him or her dirt and was out to exact revenge."

"I would not think a state senator capable of

stirring such strong reactions," Wolfe observed.

"You would be surprised—maybe *shocked* is a better word—at the number of inane and weird calls and letters that we get in the office from constituents who think their senator is also their personal problem solver. Just a few weeks ago, a woman from up in Dutchess County kept me on the phone for fifteen minutes badgering me about why Orson couldn't use his influence to get the road in front of her house paved with asphalt. When I tried to explain what the proper channels were for such work, she screamed, 'And to think that I actually voted for that man!' as she slammed the phone down.

"That was just one example. Another time—"

"I get the point," Wolfe cut in. "May I assume you have no further thoughts on the killing?"

"No, I don't," Davies said, looking sheepish. "Sorry."

"Archie, escort this gentleman to the front room and bring in Mr. Musgrove."

CHAPTER 16

Keith Musgrove edged into the office warily, as if expecting a trapdoor to open and drop him into the basement. His eyes, magnified by those thick lenses, darted from left to right and back again before settling on the substantial figure of Nero Wolfe. "I am . . . Keith Musgrove," he said in an apologetic tone that suggested we must have been expecting someone of greater importance.

"Mr. Musgrove," Wolfe said, "please be seated, and thank you for coming tonight. I trust you were served refreshments. Would you like anything more?"

"No, no, I am just fine, thank you, just fine. Your man gave me coffee, very good coffee," he said, hunching narrow shoulders as I steered him to the red leather chair. He sat on the front few inches of the cushion, kneading his hands and blinking. Maybe Fritz had served him too much coffee in the front room, or maybe he was always wound this tightly.

Wolfe waited until the pollster had ceased twitching before starting in. "I will begin by making the same request to you that I did to Mr. Davies. Please describe the events at the Polo Grounds from the moment you entered the stadium."

I won't bother feeding you a verbatim of Musgrove's report on what happened at the ball park as it essentially duplicated what Davies had told us. What you are getting here is the equivalent of an edited transcript.

"I sat on the aisle, with Todd on my right and Orson next to him," Musgrove said in his high-pitched voice. "I don't go to baseball games very often, so I was really concentrating on the action on the field, trying to learn something about strategy and such. When the home run was hit and the shot came, I probably was the last one of us aware of what had happened, as I related to the police. What followed was, well . . . I would call it pandemonium."

"Did you see Mr. Milbank fall?"

"No, no, I didn't. Todd yelled something, and that's when I turned to look. Orson was already down, with Mona and Mr. Davies bending over him. Then all sorts of other people came rushing over, some of them shoving me aside. Finally, a policeman arrived—a little late, I should say," Musgrove sniffed.

"You were the senator's pollster," Wolfe stated.

"Yes. He had been a client of mine since his first campaign for the state senate years ago."

"You have other clients?"

"Oh my, yes, I do," Musgrove said, leaning forward and finally showing some animation. "Although my firm is small—only four full-time employees, including me—we do work for several New York state assemblymen, another state senator, he's from up in Rochester, and members of the state legislatures in New Jersey and Connecticut as well. And we also do polling for various special interest groups. We are in demand, if I may say so."

"At the time of his death, what did your polls say about Senator Milbank's chances for reelection in the autumn?"

Musgrove made a clicking noise with his tongue and studied the ceiling. "The last canvass we took . . . he was running behind his opponent, getting about forty-two, forty-three percent favorable, which was up slightly from the week before. But those numbers were down from his previous campaigns, where he usually got about well over a fifty percent favorable rating. And obviously, he also got well over fifty percent of the votes cast in previous elections."

"How do you feel his position on the new road had affected his standing?" Wolfe asked.

The pollster cleared his throat and looked around the room, as if seeking an answer. "No question, his initial stance against the parkway had hurt him, and for a while we were showing support at well below forty percent, an all-time low for him. Then when he eased off on his opposition and got behind the alternate route, he jumped up a few points, and I feel that if, well . . .

if things had happened differently, in the next polls, he would have begun to move back toward fifty percent, or even above it. He had extremely strong residual respect throughout the district. I have no doubt whatever that he could have overcome the early disapproval voters had about his original position on the parkway."

"And now you will be working for Mrs. Fentress's campaign?"

"It . . . well, it has not been formally announced yet."

"Yet the candidate herself has informed Mr. Goodwin of your role," Wolfe said, "and he is by no means within her inner circle of acquaintances."

Musgrove turned red, all the way to the tips of his ears. "I don't know what to say, except that it is up to Mrs. Fentress to discuss her team with others."

"Would you consider that you have good relations with the other members of Senator Milbank's staff?"

"Overall, yes. I like to think we worked well together. Oh, there were the occasional disagreements over strategy or tactics, but these were minor differences. I felt we made a good support staff for the senator."

Wolfe shifted in his chair. "Has Mrs. Fentress selected a campaign manager?"

Musgrove appeared increasingly uncomfortable with Wolfe's questions and shook his head. "I really don't know. She has not shared her plans on that with me, and there is no reason she should."

"Do you have any theories as to who might have wanted Orson Milbank dead?"

"The police asked me that, and I told them—as I will tell you—that I have absolutely no idea. None at all."

"I thought perhaps in the process of your polling you might have encountered someone with especially rancorous feelings toward the senator."

"You've just hit upon a most interesting point," Musgrove said, sitting up straight and now energized. "We use many part-time people to make telephone calls, ring doorbells, and stop people at commuter railway stations and along streets in shopping districts. We ask these volunteers to record the reactions of voters, and almost without exception, the responses to Mr. Milbank as an individual were favorable, even from those persons who disagreed with his position on the proposed parkway and who said they definitely would vote against him. It appeared that the reservoir of good will he had amassed over the years, and which I referred to a moment ago, endeared him to the great majority of his constituents, even including those who said they definitely would vote for his opponent."

"What do you think of the anger directed at Mr. Milbank from those whom you did not canvass, specifically Messrs. Keller, Corcoran, and Bacelli?"

"Them!" Musgrove rasped, waving a hand, which for him seemed to constitute a violent gesture. "There is no question whatever that Keller in particular was angry at the senator and may have been able to sway some voters, but I've always felt that his importance as an influence on the electorate has been vastly overrated. I do not think Corcoran had much effect at all, and as for that, that *criminal,* well . . . all I can say is that I've never met him and I hope that I never will. Also, in all of our polling, we have seen nothing at all to indicate that Mr. Bacelli's opinions have any effect whatsoever on voters."

"What is your sense as to Mrs. Fentress's likelihood of winning the Milbank senate seat in the autumn?"

"It is so early in her campaign, but I firmly believe that she will emerge victorious in what likely will be a close race."

"What is her stance on the road?" Wolfe asked.

Musgrove sunk back into the red leather chair. "As I understand it, that is, well . . . yet to be determined," he said.

"Will you advise her to take a position?"

"Oh no, not at all. I do not view that as our role. We will, of course, canvass the electorate again as to their attitudes about the Northern Parkway—both its original and revised routes—and then present our findings to Mrs. Fentress. In fact, we probably will begin our polling as soon as next week. As you would expect, the candidate is eager to quickly gauge the pulse of the voters."

"Thank you for your time, sir," Wolfe said. He then turned to me, which was my cue to escort Musgrove back to the front room and fetch Todd Armstrong.

The young man seemed almost as wary as Musgrove had been as I introduced him to Wolfe and got him settled in the red leather chair. Armstrong had nothing to add to previous descriptions of the events at the baseball game, except to say that "one second, Mr. Milbank was standing next to me, the next second, he was . . . dead."

"Did you enjoy your work with the senator?" Wolfe asked.

"Yes, I did, a lot. It was a wonderful experience. I majored in political science and government at NYU and got really interested in political campaigns and all the planning that goes into them."

"What comes next for you?"

The young man shrugged and shook his head. "I really don't know for sure. When I found out Mrs. Fentress was going to run for the senate seat, I asked if she could use me on her team, but she said no, that she was going to have a very small staff and needed only people who have had a lot of experience, which I fully understood. Mr.

Davies has written me a good reference, though, and I am hoping to get a job in the office of a US Congressman. I've already sent out letters to two of them from New York and one each from Connecticut and Massachusetts, although I haven't heard anything back yet."

"Can you conceive of any reason someone would want to kill Senator Milbank?"

"No, sir, I simply cannot, and over these last several days I've given this a lot of thought. I realize, of course, that he made some people in the district angry about his position on that proposed road, but how could anyone possible commit a murder over a highway? It makes absolutely no sense to me."

"Did you ever hear anyone wish Mr. Milbank harm?"

"No—oh, wait. When the senator eased his opposition to the road, Franco Bacelli apparently made some threats, according to what I heard around the office. But I don't think anyone took them very seriously, and that includes the senator himself. One day, he even laughed with us about Bacelli's grumblings. 'That's just Franco sounding off again,' he said. 'That's to be expected of him.' "

"Did the other members of the staff seem to be concerned about Mr. Bacelli's rantings?"

Armstrong shook his head. "Not as far as I could tell. They all laughed with the senator, even Mr. Musgrove, and he hardly ever laughs."

"Before what happened to the senator, did you ever hear Mrs. Fentress express interest in holding public office?"

"No, never. I was quite surprised by her announcement, although I had not been on the staff very long, just a couple of months, so I did not know her all that well. I liked her, though. She was very friendly from my first day, and very patient helping me learn the ropes. For that matter, so was Mr. Davies."

"Very well," Wolfe said. "Now if you will excuse me, I have other business I must attend to." He rose and walked out of the office as Armstrong watched him go, a puzzled look on his face. Wolfe's destination was the kitchen, where he would likely finish off the dinner leftovers— namely, a couple of pork fillets braised in spiced wine.

"So, is that all?" he asked, turning to me.

"Yes, it is, and thank you so much for coming," I said, walking him back to the front room, where his former coworkers were thumbing through magazines.

"Now what?" Ross Davies demanded, springing to his feet.

"Now you all are free to leave," I said. "Mr. Wolfe appreciates your time."

"Although I was glad for the opportunity to meet Mr. Wolfe—and you, too, of course, it seems to me this was a total waste of time," Davies grumped. "Oh, I'm sorry, Mr. Goodwin. I guess I've just been on edge lately, after what . . . well you know. By the way, thank your man—Fritz, isn't it?—for being so solicitous toward us. The glass of wine he poured for me in the front room was absolutely first-rate. Oh, and so was the scotch, thank you."

"I will be sure to tell Fritz you liked the wine," I said as the others rose silently and followed me to the front door, where I dispatched the trio into the gentle June night and watched them walk toward Tenth Avenue, presumably in search of a taxi.

When I got to the kitchen, I found that Wolfe was tackling what had been left from dinner. He had parked himself in the only chair in that room that was big enough to accommodate him and attacked the remains of the pork fillets with gusto.

"Well?" I asked.

"Well, what?"

"Look, I know business talk is verboten during meals, but I don't count this as a meal. I call this a snack, although I concede it might look like a meal to us ordinary mortals."

Wolfe put down his utensils and glared at me. "If you insist on badgering me about the futility of this evening, you will find your efforts to be fruitless. Clearly, I learned very little from those three gentlemen that I did not already know or hadn't already surmised."

"Yeah, they weren't exactly bubbling over with new information, were they? But really, what had you hoped to get out of them?"

"I don't know, confound it! Find something to eat. This may not qualify as a meal according to your standards, but I prefer not to partake alone."

I put together some odds and ends from the refrigerator, plus a glass of milk, and sat where I usually had my breakfast. "Do I have instructions?" I posed after having done some chewing and swallowing.

"You have not heard back from Mr. Cohen about the particulars of that marine's death?"

"You know I haven't. I would have informed you."

"Surely he will report tomorrow," Wolfe said, finishing the remains of the meal. "Then there will be instructions."

CHAPTER 17

Sure enough, Lon called a few minutes before nine the next morning, just after I had settled in at my desk following breakfast. "What have you got for me today, scribe?" I asked.

"I called the mortuary this morning, where I talked to a loose-lipped employee. It turns out the young marine was a suicide."

"You have got my undivided attention. Go on."

"Unfortunately, suicides of veterans are not all that rare, as you know. A lot of them came home with their brains all messed up, which isn't surprising given the horrors they saw. Sometimes they dwell on what they've been through for years after the war and finally decide to end it all. You may remember that we did a long series on the subject in the *Gazette* a few months back, more than four years after the end of the war."

"Yeah, I do recall it. But the timing of this, given the guy was such a good marksman . . ."

"I still think it's a reach, Archie."

"How did Thompson die?"

"Shot himself with his old service revolver, or so the gabby guy at the mortuary told me."

"Where did this happen?"

"At his widowed sister's house in Queens,

Flushing to be precise. He had been living there, apparently for some time."

"Her name is Hackman, according to the death notice," I said. "I assume he was either a bachelor or divorced."

"Bachelor, never married. Again, that's according to the mortuary man, who would have given me his own life story if I had asked him for it."

"Well, after all, who else does that poor guy have to talk to? Anything more you want to tell me?"

"No, I pumped our gossipy undertaker's assistant dry. Where do you go from here?" Lon asked.

"That is up to the man who signs my checks."

"How could I forget? You will, of course, remember to keep your old and dear friend apprised as to developments."

"I'm sure that if I forget, you will remind me."

"You can bet on it," Lon said. After hanging up, I called Wolfe in the plant rooms.

"Yes?" As usual, his tone was abrupt. He hates interruptions when he is playing with his posies.

"Mr. Cohen just telephoned with further information regarding the death of Richard Thompson."

"Can it wait?"

When I responded in the affirmative, the reply was the familiar click of a line gone dead.

At one minute after eleven, Wolfe stepped into the office as if we hadn't spoken a word to each other since the night before, asking if I had slept well. Getting the pleasantries out of the way, he settled into his favorite chair, and rang for beer.

He leafed through the day's mail I had stacked on his desk blotter, then turned to me. "Report."

I proceeded to give him a verbatim account of my conversation with Lon. He leaned back saying nothing, eyes closed and hands interlaced over his stomach. Part of me hoped he would begin to push his lips in and out, in and out. That is an exercise he often—although not always— goes through on his way to solving a case. However there would be no such routine today. He opened his eyes and fastened them on me.

"That woman in Queens."

"Who are you talking about—oh, the sister of the guy who shot himself?"

"Yes. See her."

"She may not want to talk to me—or to anyone else, for that matter. And I wouldn't blame her, given all that's happened."

"Archie, there are myriad areas in which you are found to be lacking, areas we have often discussed. However, resourcefulness is not among them, and I have never known you to shy away from a challenge. I have full confidence you will find a way to ingratiate yourself with Mrs. Hackman."

"You remember her name?"

"Certainly," Wolfe said, sending me one of those looks I get whenever he thinks I underestimate him.

• • •

Several years ago, because I thought it would help with a case we were working on, I had a phony press card made up, never mind how. It sports a photograph of my phiz with a properly serious expression and identifies me as a staff reporter for a major New York newspaper—but not the *Gazette*, in deference to my friendship with Lon Cohen. I had never used the card, feeling that was one line I preferred not to cross, and even Wolfe was unaware of its existence.

I took the card from the top dresser drawer in my room, admiring my likeness in the photo. The card identified me as ALAN G. NELSON, REPORTER. Why Alan G. Nelson, you ask? A common name, but not too common, like Joe Smith or John Jones. I slipped the card into a slot in my billfold and went downstairs to join Wolfe for lunch in the dining room, veal cutlets and Fritz's best mixed salad with Devil's Rain dressing, followed by a rhubarb tart.

After polishing off the meal, we went to the office and had coffee. While Wolfe immersed himself in one of his current books, *The Universe and Dr. Einstein* by Lincoln Barnett, I dialed the number listed for Marguerite Hackman of Queens, hoping she was not at work. A listless female voice answered on the third ring.

"Mrs. Hackman?"

"Yes, I am Marguerite Hackman. But if you are

selling something, forget it, because I am not buying."

I assured her I was not a pitchman and identified my so-called self and my newspaper, saying I was doing a feature on war heroes and their difficulties in adjusting to civilian life.

"I really am not interested, Mr. Nelson."

"But your brother was a true hero."

"Yes, yes, he was, but he was not the same man when he came back," she said in a voice full of unutterable sadness.

"I would like to come to your home if I may, Mrs. Hackman, and learn about your brother and his struggles." I could hear breathing on the other end for five seconds, ten, fifteen.

"You say that you are a newspaper reporter?"

"Yes," I told her, repeating the name of the newspaper and wondering if this was the lie that would finally consign me to the fires of hell that I had learned about in Sunday school as a kid growing up back in the Ohio farming country.

More breathing, then a sigh. "All right. Now mind you, I don't have guests in my house often, so please do not expect anything fancy."

"No, ma'am, I won't. I'm hardly the fancy type myself. When would it be convenient for me to see you?"

"Oh, dear, let me see. What about this evening? Would seven thirty be all right for you?" I told her I'd be there, cradling the receiver and making a mental note to request that Fritz save me a serving of the shrimp bordelaise that was on the dinner menu.

At a few minutes before seven, I stepped out into the evening sun and walked toward Tenth Avenue to flag a northbound cab. I usually have a sense of anyone tailing me, and after I had gone no more than twenty paces from the brownstone, I realized a car, a light-gray Chevrolet sedan, was moving along slowly behind me. At the corner, I hailed a yellow cab and jumped in. "See that Chevy?" I told the driver, who looked like he could have seen action in the First World War.

"Don't tell me, let me guess," he said with a lopsided grin. "You want me to lose him, right?"

"You somehow read my mind. Think you can?"

He laughed hoarsely. "Hell, I could shake a boa constrictor, sport. Hang on. By the way, just where we headed?"

I gave him the address. "Flushing, huh? I'll be damned. Every other time I've gone to that part of town has been to take fares out to LaGuardia, as they're calling our airport nowadays." He floored his hack as we lurched up Tenth Avenue, weaving from one lane to another and back again amid the honking from drivers we had cut off. "Chevy still behind us?" he asked.

I looked out the back window. "I don't see it, but keep going as if it was still right behind us."

By the time we crossed the Fifty-Ninth Street Bridge and entered Long Island City, I was sure we had lost the tail, and I sat back, silently rehearsing my interview with Marguerite Hackman.

"You can drop me here," I told the cabbie when we had traversed the streets of Queens and reached the neighborhood. "This is close enough."

"What? We're still more than a block from where you're going. Don't you believe I shook him?"

"People in my line of work can't be too careful," I said, realizing I sounded like an actor in a Grade-B gangster film. "But you did do one hell of a job," I added, giving him a healthy tip.

CHAPTER 18

I walked along the tree-lined street past almost identical two-story frame houses that stood shoulder to shoulder with only narrow passageways separating them. My destination differed from its neighbors only in that its shutters were a bright yellow as opposed to the black of almost every other house.

The woman in a housedress who opened the door to my knock was probably close to forty, but her drawn appearance added years and her thin smile was forced, accenting the lines on her face. "I am Marguerite Hackman, Mr. Nelson. Please come in," she said softly. "I hope you were able to find the house easily."

"I was, thank you," I said, showing her my press card and stepping into a small, neat living room with green-and-white striped wallpaper, a sofa, two chairs, and a small television set with a round screen in one corner. Framed photographs of two men shared a mahogany end table, the younger one in uniform and wearing a somber expression, the older man in a double-breasted business suit and smiling. I liked his looks.

"Please sit down," Mrs. Hackman said. "I've just brewed a fresh pot of coffee. Will you have a cup?"

I told her that would be fine and sat at one end of the sofa, pulling out a pencil and my reporter's notebook. "That was Richard—Dick he was always called," she said when she returned with a coffeepot and two cups on a tray. She indicated the marine, who looked sternly out from the photograph. "The other picture is of my late husband, Earl, who died four years ago of cancer, much too young. He had just turned forty-two when he was taken from me.

"Our one regret was that we were never able to have children," she went on, "but our marriage was wonderful nonetheless. I wouldn't have changed a minute of it."

I studied both photos and nodded. "So you have lost the two men closest to you. That's rough."

"Yes, it is," she said, sitting in one of the chairs and smoothing the skirt of her housedress. "They were very different, Earl and Dick," she went on as she poured coffee. "My husband was outgoing, friendly, always ready with a joke or a story. He was a grand storyteller. Just the type to be a salesman, which he was. He enjoyed life and he enjoyed meeting people. He represented a company that made small kitchen appliances, like toasters, waffle irons, and orange juice squeezers, and he sold them to department stores and hardware stores in the New York area, including over in New Jersey and the close-by towns in Connecticut. That meant he never had to travel.

He was home every night, usually with lively tales about the events of his day." I nodded as I sipped the very good coffee.

"My brother—he was eleven years younger than me—was quite a different story, Mr. Nelson. He was always wild, from even before his high school days. He got thrown out of school at least twice, never got a high school diploma, and my parents finally told him to get out of the house. He enlisted in the marines even before Pearl Harbor, and—did you read the death notice in one of your competing papers, the *Gazette*?"

"Yes, I did. That's where I learned about Dick."

"Then, of course, you know the details of his heroism," she said. "I don't think he even fired cap guns as a kid. But in the marines, he became an excellent shot and won all kinds of awards during training, even before he got into the war."

"Your parents must have been very proud of what he did on Okinawa."

"They were proud of him, although they both died within a few months of each other soon after the Japanese surrender, so they saw very little of Dick after the war. Which was a good thing."

"Why do you say that?" I asked as I went through the motions of scribbling in my notebook.

"The war had a terrible effect on Dick," she murmured. "He wasn't the same man when he came back. Oh, I don't mean because of his physical injury, which was minor—shrapnel in his legs, which got removed in a military hospital before he came home. It was his mental injuries that really changed him. He had developed a bad stutter, and he started drinking a lot. He had never been much of a drinker before, even in his wild days. But that was not the worst of it."

"Oh?"

"Back home, he began hanging out with a bad crowd. Some of them were veterans, too, and overall they were a mean bunch. Although I couldn't prove it, I think he began using some sort of drugs around the time. He lived alone in my parents' house over in Jamaica after they died and he threw some wild parties there. The neighbors on all sides complained, and that brought in the police. Dick started a fight with one of the officers and ended up spending a night in jail."

"Was he working at the time?"

"Off and on. He had a number of jobs, so many I lost count. He unloaded ships on the North River docks for a few weeks but got fired. Same with construction work and day labor. He even worked for a while at both Yankee Stadium and the Polo Grounds doing janitorial work, but he lost those jobs, too. He was undependable."

"Was it well known that he had been such a great marksman?"

"Yes, it was. A year or so ago, you may remember that the *Gazette* did a series of articles on honored war veterans living in and around

New York, including the suburban areas. They called it 'The Heroes Among Us' and featured a different marine, soldier, sailor, or airman every day for months. The write-up on Dick included a picture of him holding his rifle. It was taken in this room by a *Gazette* photographer. I was right here when it happened. After the series was finished, the newspaper held a fancy dinner at one of the big hotels, the Waldorf Astoria, it was, honoring each of the men and including all kinds of politicians and executives in the audience. I even helped Dick buy a new suit for the occasion."

"He must have felt pretty good about that."

"He didn't seem too excited about it before-hand, although I think he had a pretty good time, meeting those other GIs and comparing stories."

"Did he ever get married?"

"No, and that, too, is a very sad story. As you can see from his picture, Dick was a handsome young man. There were several girls interested in him. One in particular, her name was Ellen, would have been good for Dick, a steadying influence. She knew him before the war, but like a lot of us, she saw an entirely different person when he came home. I think he was incapable of any sort of permanent relationship by then. They saw each other off and on, but Ellen finally realized it was not going to work out."

"Did your brother ever get any kind of psychiatric help?"

"He wouldn't hear of it," she said, clenching a small fist and pounding her knee. "He insisted there was nothing at all wrong with him. I brought the subject up only once, and he threw a fit. He started screaming and telling me to mind my own business."

"Had anything else about him changed after he came home from the war?"

She looked down at her lap and seemed to be composing herself. "I know this is hard," I said.

She nodded. "As I said before, Dick was totally different, and not at all for the better. He had always had a temper, but he lost it much more quickly after he came home. The fight that landed him in jail was an example, the worst one."

"Did he keep on living in your parents' house?"

"Not for long after that time when the police came and took him away. We sold the place and split the proceeds, not that there was all that much to divvy up. Dick then moved into one of those cheap hotels over on the Upper West Side of Manhattan until his money ran out. I always suspected he spent it on alcohol and drugs, especially drugs."

"How did he happen to move in with you?"

Marguerite's sad face became even sadder. "After Earl died, I was alone here, of course. Oh, I was by no means destitute, not at all. Earl had a pension from his company, and that has been more than sufficient for my needs. But Dick begged me to let him move in. 'You've got plenty of space here, Sis,' he had said, 'and I won't be any trouble, I promise.'

"I gave in, which was a mistake, Mr. Nelson. Dick had his room upstairs all right, which in itself was fine, but his friends, if you can call them that, came to visit—and to drink in this very room. Now I am not a teetotaler, Mr. Nelson, but I did not want to see my house, the home my husband and I had lived in so happily for almost fifteen years, turned into some sort of cheap saloon full of rowdies. I told Dick how unhappy I was with the people he hung around with, and he became apologetic and—what is the word?—contrite, I think. He told me the visits to our house would stop. And they did, except for another kind of visit."

"Please go on, Mrs. Hackman."

"What I am going to tell you happened only quite recently, no more than a month or so ago. Would you like more coffee?"

"No, thank you. These visits?"

She chewed on her lower lip. "A man telephoned here, asking for Dick. He wasn't home at the time and I asked if I could take a message, but he would not leave his name and said he would call again."

"Did he?"

She nodded. "Dick became very secretive about this individual. He came to the house just once,

183

and Dick insisted I go upstairs to my room and close the door."

"So you never saw this mystery man?"

"Only from my bedroom window, which looks down on the street. It was after dark, and I watched as he came up to the front door. There was just enough light from a street lamp for me to see that he had a wide-brimmed hat on, pulled low over his face."

"And you have no idea at all about what this individual's business was with your brother?"

"No, but whatever it was got Dick very excited, or maybe *agitated* is a better word. He then told me that something big was going to happen. That's what he said, 'Something big, something that will let me move out of here, out of your hair for good, into my own place, a nice place.' The man called again several times, and it was obvious to me that he was behind these plans. Whatever they were, I believe it had to do with . . . what happened to Dick later." She looked down at her lap again and sniffed, but no tears came.

"Would you be able to identify this man?"

"Not by a face, I wouldn't. But I'm sure that I would recognize his voice. I heard it at least three, maybe four times on the telephone. It was distinctive, although I don't know exactly how to describe it."

"Could I take a look at your brother's room?"

"Why not? There's really not much to see." I

followed Marguerite up a narrow stairway to a narrow, wallpapered hall. She pushed open a door and stepped aside to let me enter. There certainly wasn't much to see: a window that looked out onto the backyard, a single bed in one corner, a maple dresser topped by an oval mirror, a marine poster tacked on the wall, and a closet.

"Your brother won a lot of awards and medals," I said. "I expected to seem them displayed."

"He got rid of all of them, sold the bunch, or so he told me. At that time of his life, it seemed he'd do anything to get a few dollars," she said.

I opened the closet door, hearing no objection. "I got rid of all of his clothes," Marguerite explained, "gave them to the Salvation Army. I felt they should be put to use. Not much else in there, I'm afraid."

But there was something. Leaning against a wall at the back of the closet was a rifle, an M1 Garand. "This was your brother's?"

"Yes, he brought it back from the service. I don't know if he was supposed to do that, but he came home with it and also with a pistol, the gun he . . . he killed himself with."

"Did he have a particular reason to keep firearms around?"

"Do you mean, was he afraid of anyone? I really don't think so. I believe he held on to the weapons as keepsakes, strange as that seems to me. After he got rid of his medals, they were all that was left to remind him of the war, although I don't know why he would want to be reminded."

"Where did the shooting take place, Mrs. Hackman?"

"Right here, right in this very room," she said, pointing to the floor. "I was downstairs at the time and heard the shot. Just one shot . . . to the head. I found him on the floor, right there. He was gone. That awful sight will stay with me the rest of my days."

"Did he leave a note?"

"No, nothing, not a single word. He had been unusually depressed those last few days, although I don't know why. He would barely speak to me. I remember one call in particular from that man. After Dick hung up, he was almost hysterical, and that night . . . well, that was when it happened."

"Can you recall the exact date?"

She frowned. "Yes, of course, I can. However could I possibly forget? It was June 14."

"Flag Day. What became of the pistol?"

"The police took it. 'A formality,' they said. I should have told them to take the rifle away, too. I certainly do not need it as a memory of Dick."

"My advice is that you hold on to that rifle for now," I said to her. "I have my reasons. Did you find anything unusual among his personal effects?"

"No, not really. His dresser was full of clothes, as one would expect, nothing else. Oh, well, there was one thing that seemed a little strange. In the top drawer of the chest, I found his key ring, but with two large keys on it that I did not recognize."

"Really? Is it still here?"

"Yes, in the drawer, right where I left it," Marguerite said, motioning to the dresser.

"May I see it?"

She shrugged and nodded, opening the drawer and handing me the ring. "Those two are for the front and back doors of this house," she said, pointing to the smaller keys, "but the large ones . . . I have no idea at all."

"Do you think that he was in the habit of taking keys from places where he had worked?"

"Again, I don't have any idea. Are you suggesting something criminal, like maybe Dick would go back to these workplaces and steal things?"

"I'm not suggesting anything," I said. "Mind if I take the mystery keys?" She shook her head and I took them off the ring. They were not identical, but both were thick and heavy, clearly designed for opening large doors . . . or perhaps gates.

Marguerite shot a puzzled look my way as we went down the stairs to the first floor. "Is there anything else you need to know?" she asked.

"No, I don't think so, at least not for the time being," I said as I pulled open the front door. "Thank you so much for your hospitality."

"You really are not a newspaperman, are you, Mr. Nelson? And is Nelson even your name?"

"What makes you ask?"

"Your questions, for one thing. They did not seem to focus nearly as much on my brother's mental state as they did on his recent actions, and on that man he had dealings with just before he died. And also your wanting to take those keys."

I ignored her comments about the keys. "Aren't you curious about that man yourself, Mrs. Hackman?"

"Of course, I am, Mr. . . . whatever your name is. But I am also curious about you, very curious."

"I wish I could say more now, but I'm sorry that I cannot."

She looked at me, unblinking. "For some strange reason, I trust you."

"I'm glad to know that. I promise you will be hearing from me again." With that, I turned and went down the front steps into the darkness.

CHAPTER 19

As I walked away from the house, I silently berated myself for not doing a better job at playing a reporter and also for not having that taxi wait for me at the corner where I got dropped off. I retraced my steps toward the intersection in hopes of hailing another cab and had gone almost a block when I realized there were footfalls several paces behind me. A neighborhood resident walking a dog? I stopped and the footsteps stopped. I started, and they started.

Wishing I had taken one of the guns from the safe in the office, I wheeled around and faced my tail. That's not all I faced. A stocky man in a snap-brim hat and black sport coat was holding an automatic pointed at me.

"You lost us there for a time, Mr. Private Eye, but we got the number of your hack and found him. With a little bit of persuasion, we got the cabbie to tell us where he dropped you off, and we've been waiting for you."

"What did you do to the guy?" I snapped.

The answer was a hoarse laugh. "We didn't do nothin' to him, pal, except cross his palm with a finif. That got him talkin'. What did ya think, that maybe we knocked him around? Hell, we didn't

189

need to. Our money did the talking." Another laugh with no humor behind it.

"And we ain't gonna knock you around, neither, pal, as long as you tell us where you just been. That right, Lenny?"

"Right," came a voice from behind me. So much for my keen sense of knowing when I was being shadowed. I turned and saw a taller man, also wearing a snap-brim hat and topcoat and holding a snub-nosed revolver. Definitely not a good sign.

"So, how about letting us in on where you've just been at," the one called Lenny said.

"I don't have any idea what the hell you're talking about," I said, trying to sound tough.

"Aw, don't be that way," Lenny said, walking up to me and driving a fist into my gut. I doubled over and groaned as the stocky one gave me a kick in the kidneys. I was on the pavement now, in a fetal position.

At that moment, I heard a familiar voice. "Hardly a fair fight, is it, boys? Now put down those silly toys of yours. I have one of my own, and it's got a silencer, as you can see. I could finish both of you off right here on this quiet Flushing street, and nobody would ever be the wiser. You boys probably know that stuff like that happens all the time. Now let me hear those guns hit the concrete."

The men dropped their weapons as I got to my feet with a groan. "Wise choice, fellas," Saul

Panzer said. "Nice to see you've got some sense. Now turn your backs to me, both of you, hands up nice and high."

"Damn, you can't shoot us like this," Lenny pleaded. Interesting how the tone of his voice had changed in the last minute.

"Oh, I don't think I'll plug you," Saul said, "although I must say it's damned tempting. Archie, I brought another piece for you." He smiled and handed me my Marley .38. "Now let's wrap these boys up, shall we?" He pulled two sets of handcuffs from his topcoat pocket. "Okay, you," he said to Lenny, "give me your right paw." When he resisted, Saul jammed the barrel of his revolver into the gunman's ear. "I really don't want to splatter your brains on this nice peaceful street, but I will if you don't give me a choice."

Lenny held out his hand, which was shaking. Saul snapped a cuff on him. "Now you, what's your name?" Saul barked at the other man.

"Tony," the short one answered in a surly tone.

"Okay, Mr. Tony, let's have your left hand—now!" Saul took the other half of the cuffs, and now the hoods were linked. He then opened the second set of cuffs, put one bracelet on Tony's right hand and the other he snapped around the iron pole that held up a NO PARKING sign.

"There, now you are all set to welcome the men from the local precinct," Saul said, picking up their guns and emptying the bullets out of each, then dumping them through a grating into the sewer and putting the weapons on the pavement near their feet. "See you boys around."

"You sons of bitches," Lenny howled. "You'll pay for this."

"I don't think so," Saul said. "And that's not a very smart thing to say to someone who has a weapon pointed at you. Archie, I didn't see a police call-box along here, but there is a phone booth at the corner. Let's go."

As we walked away from the tethered hoods, I grabbed Saul's arm. "You don't look much like a guardian angel. How in heaven's name did you happen to be here?"

"Mr. Wolfe was concerned that you might get tailed, so I ended up shadowing the shadowers."

"How did you get my Marley?"

"I was in the front room with the door closed when you left. I went to the office, pulled your trusty .38 from the safe, and was out on the street just in time to see that Chevy tailing you. After you jumped into a cab with them behind, I grabbed my own yellow."

"Gee, a regular parade. What fun."

"It sure was. Whoa, speaking of their car," Saul said as we came upon the gray Chevy parked at the curb. "Let's give them something more to remember about this evening. He drew out the pistol with the silencer and fired one shot into the sedan's right front tire, smiling as the car settled down on its rim.

"You play pretty rough," I said, grinning.

"Damn right, especially when somebody tries to mess with my friend Archie Goodwin. But if I had been really angry, I would have popped all four tires just for the fun of it. Here's the phone booth," Saul said, stepping in. "I just happen to have the phone number of the 109th Precinct handy, along with the coin of the realm."

He dropped a nickel in the phone, dialed, and spoke into the mouthpiece. "Yes Sergeant, this is a concerned citizen. My name is not important. If you're interested, you will find two ruffians chained together on 115th Street—just north of Fourteenth Avenue—and anchored to a pole holding up a NO PARKING sign. They were playing with guns, but it seems that a couple of pensioners passing by didn't like that and disarmed them. Where in the world these old men could have got the handcuffs, I really don't know." Saul hung up and stepped out of the booth.

"Okay, let's find us a cab," he said. "You feeling okay?"

"I've been better," I said, running as hand over my stomach and my sore back. "It's a good thing that I haven't eaten dinner, because if I had, it would be all over the street where those apes slugged me. So, did you have trouble keeping pace during that chase into Queens?"

"My cabbie kept the Chevy in sight all the way. They lost you but must have got your cabbie's number, because they pulled him over later and one of the goons handed him some dough."

"A fiver," I said. "But they didn't know exactly where I was because I got off more than a block from my destination. I'll fill you in more on that later. You figure these were Bacelli's boys?"

"Yeah, almost surely," Saul said. "Hey, here's a cab. Let's head back to peaceful old Manhattan." He gave Wolfe's address and we hopped in. Our taxi hadn't gone more than a block when a black-and-white screamed past us in the opposite direction with lights flashing and siren blaring. "I'd love to be an onlooker when a couple of New York's Best find those two knuckleheads chained together," I said as we sped through Queens on our way back to Manhattan. "It will be the talk of the station house for months to come."

"Yeah, and imagine how one Franco Bacelli is going to react when he finds out about how his boys managed to mess up," Saul said. "You know, I played with the idea of taking their wallets and their guns, but I figured, why rile up the Mafia's top dog any more than necessary? These two plug-uglies will already be in enough trouble with the Mob higher-ups."

"True. As it is, I'll lay odds that Nero Wolfe will soon be hearing from Bacelli. You may not be

194

aware of this, but the Syndicate's big man visited the brownstone just yesterday, offering to join forces to find out who killed Milbank."

"An offer that Mr. Wolfe, of course, refused," Saul said.

"Of course. Bacelli, who claimed to have all kinds of sources, stormed off saying he would find the killer and screw Wolfe out of his fee."

Saul laughed. "And it turns out Bacelli's so-called 'source' was none other than you. He figured if he put a tail on you that would lead him—or in this case his thick-skulled flunkies—to the answer."

"I did some dumb things tonight, but my one smart move was getting the cabbie to drop me off more than a block from where I was headed."

"Sometimes, one smart move is all it takes, Archie."

"I guess so. Say, another question: How did you happen to be toting two sets of handcuffs? I didn't know they were part of your usual baggage."

"They're not. For some reason, maybe an inkling of things to come, I grabbed them out of the safe in your office when I got the Marley," Saul said, shaking his head ruefully. "Glad you brought it up, Archie. I'll have to reimburse Mr. Wolfe for them."

"The hell you will. If anybody's going to pay to replace those bracelets, it's me, after the stupid stunt I pulled."

"We can talk about it later. Here we are," Saul said as the taxi pulled up in front of the brownstone.

Wolfe was reading when we walked into the office. "Are you hurt?" he said, looking up and eyeing me.

"My body a little, my pride a lot," I told him, sliding gingerly into the chair behind my desk and wincing. "Fortunately, this gentleman's timing was impeccable," I said, nodding in Saul's direction. "I suppose I should be irked that you felt I needed looking after, but under the circumstances, well . . ."

Wolfe set his book down. "It would seem you have earned a drink, Saul," he said. "You know where to find the scotch."

"I do, and a fine label it is. Thank you, sir."

"What about me?"

"Since when have you ever bothered to ask?" Wolfe posed.

"Point taken," I said, asking Saul to get me a scotch from the bar cart against the wall, which he did. "I assume you want a report?"

Wolfe dipped his head a quarter of an inch, the signal to proceed.

For the next half hour, Saul and I recounted the events of the evening, from our respective trips over to Queens to my visit with Marguerite Hackman and the face-off with the pair of toughs who were presumably in the employ of Franco

Bacelli. Wolfe took it all in, along with two bottles of beer.

"Oh, and one other thing," I told him, purposely saving my little surprise for last. "Thompson's sister found these on his key ring when she was going through his personal effects. She had no explanation for them." I dumped the pair of keys on his blotter.

"Most unusual," Wolfe said, picking them up and studying them. "Also most suggestive." He leaned back and closed his eyes for several minutes while we sat in silence, finishing our drinks.

"Saul, I thank you again for your service tonight," he said after his brief séance. "It would seem that Archie is in your debt. Perhaps he can show his appreciation by having you as his guest some evening at Rusterman's."

"Funny, I was just thinking the same thing," Saul said, grinning and getting to his feet. "Well, I've had all the excitement I want for one day. I will say goodnight."

After Saul had left, Wolfe turned to me. "I hardly think instructions are necessary concerning these keys, or at least one of them."

"A visit to the Polo Grounds," I said.

Wolfe nodded, then made a face. "I can almost guarantee that Inspector Cramer will be here tomorrow, probably in the morning," he said. "Archie, go to bed, get some rest." With that, he rose, left the office, and headed for the elevator.

CHAPTER 20

As usual, Wolfe had nailed it. The next morning following his session with the orchids, the world's smartest detective had been at his desk less than ten minutes when the doorbell rang. "Per your prediction, it's you-know-who," I said after walking down the hall and viewing the stocky figure on the stoop through the one-way glass. "Do I let him in?"

I got the hint of a nod along with a scowl and went to the front door, pulling it open. "You are late," I told Cramer, looking at my watch. "Since he's been downstairs, he's already had time to order beer and drink almost half of the first bottle." The glowering inspector refused to look at me and said nothing, brushing on by and stomping toward the office.

"Good morning, sir," Wolfe said evenly.

"I'll tell you if and when it's good," Cramer gruffed, dropping into the red leather chair, pulling out a cigar, and jamming it into his mouth. "And it sure as hell isn't a good morning right now."

"May I assume you are referring to the Milbank case?"

"You may. By chance, have you seen today's *Mirror*?"

"No, sir. That is not one of the newspapers delivered here."

"Of course—what was I thinking?" Cramer said, slapping his forehead. "That tabloid is way too low-brow for the likes of you two. Well, here is what you missed by being elitists: a page one editorial, with a headline in red type, no less. Leave that kind of stunt to the Hearst crowd. Anyhow, the paper has topped the *Daily News*'s reward of fifty grand for information leading to the arrest and conviction of Orson Milbank's killer by offering seventy-five thousand dollars themselves."

"The press has indeed been exhibiting commendable civic responsibility," Wolfe said.

"Commendable civic responsibility, my aunt Fanny!" Cramer bellowed. "That latest reward was a flamboyant way of underscoring the editorial's main point, which is what they refer to as, and I quote, 'the sorry state of law enforcement in this great metropolis.'"

"Strong words."

"Oh, there's more, lots more. Their diatribe goes on to say, and I can recite every word, that 'it is a tragedy of immense proportions that the police department of the nation's largest and most important city also happens to be the nation's worst and most inept police department. Perhaps we should formally rename them the Keystone Kops.' The editorial then singles out Commissioner

Humbert and yours truly for special mention. 'Both of these men are taking their salaries under false pretenses' is how we are presented."

"I am sorry to hear that, at least the mention of your name in that context," Wolfe said, sounding as if he meant it. "My views on the commissioner, however, are well known."

"Oh, that's just the beginning," Cramer replied, chewing on his unlit stogie. "You can bet that now the other papers will try to top the *Mirror* with bigger rewards and even stronger blasts at the department—and at me. Well, I can live with the heat. God knows, I have for years; it comes with the job. And if they do decide to throw me out on my tail, as I have been expecting, so be it. But I didn't come here to complain about myself. Something unusual happened last night, and I would be interested in your thoughts."

"Indeed? You rarely solicit my opinion, sir," Wolfe said, coming forward in his chair. "Should I be flattered?"

Cramer grunted. "Not necessarily. Maybe it simply says something about my state of mind these days. I'm well aware that your knowledge of the city's geography has never been one of your strong points, so I will go slow. Do you happen to know where Flushing is?"

"Somewhere over in Queens, I believe."

"Bingo. It has the airport, of course, but in general it is a quiet area, residential streets with some trees, single-family homes, hardworking people, and very few troublemakers."

"An idyllic picture," Wolfe agreed.

"Yeah, so one would think. But last night, the boys from one of the local precincts over there got a strange, anonymous phone call. The voice on the line said that two men were handcuffed together on a corner, and one of them also was handcuffed to a signpost. The caller also claimed they had been disarmed and cuffed by a couple of pensioners—not very likely."

"A most unusual occurrence."

"Yeah, isn't it, though? Things get even more unusual. A prowl car tore off to the intersection and, I'll be damned, what the uniforms found was exactly what had been reported in the anonymous call: two men, cuffed together and unable to move beyond the signpost. And it doesn't stop there. These two turned out to be Lenny Packer and Tony Motta, a couple of thugs on the payroll, or so we think, of one Franco Bacelli. Strange, wouldn't you say?"

Wolfe raised his shoulders and let them drop. "I am not familiar with the intricacies of the world of organized crime, so I cannot venture an opinion, although this does seem to be puzzling, at least on the surface."

"You can't venture an opinion, eh?" Cramer said. "Well, let me push on, if you don't mind. Bacelli and Liam Dwyer, a rival mobster whose name you may have seen in print, have been in a blood feud of late, and a number of their men have been killed, presumably by the other side. Now here we find two guys from one of the warring armies alive and well, although damned embarrassed. Their guns, a snub-nosed revolver and an automatic, were found lying in the street beside them, chambers empty. The pistols had not been fired, at least not recently. Don't you find that strange?"

"It does seem somewhat out of the ordinary," Wolfe said. "What did Messrs. Packer and Motta say by way of explanation?"

"Not a blessed word!" Cramer said. "They just asked for a lawyer, who happens to be with them now. The lawyer is a Bacelli mouthpiece, hardly a surprise. There's nothing we can really hold them on, except unlicensed possession of a weapon. Oh, and one other thing: The automobile in which they had apparently traveled to the area was found nearby with one of its tires ripped apart like it had been shot, which it had. A shell casing was found on the pavement under the car.

"Now bear in mind, this is a peaceful neighborhood, one of the quietest in the whole damned city. There hasn't even been a car theft within blocks in more than two years. Oh, and—as I said earlier—our anonymous caller claimed the hoods had been disarmed by a couple of old men who were passing by and didn't like having them in the neighborhood. Preposterous."

"All very interesting, Inspector. But why are you telling us about this?" Wolfe asked.

"Sometimes I'm a little slow on the uptake, but I got curious and began wondering if somehow, some way, these strange goings-on were tied to the death of Milbank. I just thought I'd see if you had any thoughts."

"Archie," Wolfe said, turning to me, "have you any theories about this admittedly strange occurrence?"

"None, but if I were to guess, it would be that these two cretins found their way into Flushing and decided to cause some trouble. Why . . . I don't know. They may have run into not old men but rather some young neighborhood guys who turned out to be tougher than these hoods thought and the young men decided to teach them a lesson without really hurting them. Then to rub it in, when they called the precinct, they said the hoods had been disarmed by a couple of old-timers."

"Young neighborhood guys who just happened to have handcuffs and were able to disarm two hard cases?" Cramer posed. "Also preposterous. And who shot the hoods' tire?"

I shrugged. "Sorry. I gave the only explanation I can think of."

"It would seem that given the way you have described Flushing, it would be an unlikely place to have any connection with the senator's murder," Wolfe said.

"So it would seem," Cramer agreed grudgingly. "By the way, have you made any progress on your investigation?"

"Very little. And you?"

"Hah! Next to nothing. We've interviewed probably fifty or sixty people who were in the Polo Grounds that afternoon, including ushers, vendors, groundskeepers, and even the radio broadcaster, and not one of them noticed a single soul in the left-field upper deck."

"That is hardly a place anybody would look unless a ball headed out that way," I said.

"That's just it!" Cramer growled. "A ball *did* head out that way—the home run that got hit just before the shooting."

"Yes, but remember that the homer sailed into the lower deck, Inspector," I said. "In fact, it just barely cleared the wall. It looked like the left fielder might be able to grab it, so everybody's attention was focused there, not upstairs where you say the shooter apparently was."

Cramer shot me a glare. "You've got yourself an answer for just about everything, don't you?"

"We realize you have been under a great deal of pressure, sir," Wolfe put in, "but what Mr. Goodwin said makes perfect sense. I am hardly an authority on baseball, but all eyes would have been focused on the ball and the player trying to catch it, wouldn't they?"

"Yeah, that well may be. It's certainly not

getting us any closer to putting this mess to rest." As he got up to leave, he stuck his chewed-over cigar into the breast pocket of his suit jacket. That alone said volumes about his mental state. He usually ended his visits to the brownstone in a rage, hurling the stogie at our wastebasket and invariably missing.

"Oh, one more thing, Goodwin," Cramer said as he paused in the office doorway. "Were you by chance in Flushing last night?"

"Flushing is hardly a place I am accustomed to visiting. I've probably been there no more than once or twice in my life."

The burly copper mouthed a word and steamed off down the hall. After he had gone and I had locked the front door behind him, I went back to the office, where Wolfe was reading his book. "Well, I did not lie to the man," I said.

"No, that much can be said. Mr. Cramer finds himself stuck up a tree without a ladder."

"I don't see that we're all that much better off ourselves."

"At the moment, we are not, although we do not have government officials, civic organizations, and outraged journalists ranting about our ineptitude and clamoring for our jobs."

"Well, at the moment, I have to say that I'm feeling pretty damned inept myself. What's next?"

Wolfe started to reply when the phone rang. I

answered, and a now-familiar voice asked for Nero Wolfe.

I turned to Wolfe and silently mouthed the caller's name, staying on the line. He picked up the receiver. "Yes?"

"I believe you know who this is."

"I do. State your business."

"Your boys like to play pretty rough," Franco Bacelli said.

"Only when they are given no alternative. If you are calling to complain, I might point out that those two men whom I presume are in your employ could have had their weapons and their identification papers taken from them. As it is, they were left unbruised, which is more than I can say for an associate of mine."

"People don't mess with my men, Mr. Nero Wolfe."

"Nor with mine, sir. Your men are incompetent boobs. When you came to my home, uninvited, you boasted that you would find Senator Milbank's killer before I did. Your method, it now appears, was to follow one of my agents and determine what line he was pursuing, rather than to conduct an independent investigation of your own. You and your operatives have been badly outflanked."

"And you have made yourself an enemy and you will live to regret it," Bacelli growled.

"*Pfui!* Over the years, I have made far more formidable enemies than you, sir. Now if you have nothing more to say, I—" Wolfe stopped talking because the line had gone dead.

"Now I wish Saul and I *had* taken their guns and their identification," I said. "Then you could have demanded that Bacelli come here to pick them up."

"I have no desire to see that man more often that is absolutely necessary," Wolfe grumped. "A visit to the Polo Grounds is in order, I believe."

"Yep. Specific instructions?"

"Obviously, determine whether one or more of those keys fits into locks on the stadium gates. Avoid detection if possible."

"Well, for starters, there's no game there today; the Giants are playing down in Philadelphia, so the ball park figures to be empty, or close to it. If I do run into someone?"

"Use your intelligence, guided by experience," Wolfe replied, repeating a line he has used on me more times than I can count. Before I could attempt to fire off a clever retort, he picked up his current book and buried his nose in it, his signal for me to button my lip.

CHAPTER 21

As I mentioned earlier, the Polo Grounds lies near the northern tip of Manhattan. To be more precise, it squats like a tired and battered fortress at West 155th Street and Eighth Avenue and backs up to the Harlem River, the narrow waterway separating Manhattan and the Bronx. I parked the Heron on the street and walked over to the old park's entrance nearest home plate. Not surprisingly, the joint seemed to be shut up tight.

Seeing no one around, I strode to one of the barred iron gates and eyed its large lock. I pulled the pair of keys from my pocket, but before I could try one, a voice interrupted me.

"Hey, you there, Mac!" It was a short, red-haired guy in blue coveralls standing with a cigarette outside a gate farther along the stadium's outer wall. "The joint's closed up, unless you wanna order advance tickets," he yelled as he trotted toward me. "Those windows is around on the other side. I think at least one of them's open."

"Thanks, but I'm really looking for someone in your maintenance department," I improvised. "Anybody around?"

"Every one of our crew is out on the field now, getting it in shape for the Pittsburgh series. I was just grabbing a quick smoke on my break. Anything special you want?"

"Just to talk to the boss."

"Too bad, he ain't around. Hadda go to a funeral, his wife's aunt. But his assistant's here, the straw boss, you might call him. Follow me."

We walked along the outer wall for about twenty yards and came to an open gate. I followed him as we walked through a dank tunnel under the stands and then out onto the sunlit playing surface. There were more than a dozen men, also in blue coveralls, scattered around the diamond and the outfield with shovels, rakes, and hoses, working to pretty up one of the oldest and most historic fields in baseball.

"Hey, Marty, guy here needs to see you," the redhead shouted, pointing a thumb in my direction. A husky specimen wearing a sport coat and a broad-brimmed hat turned from supervising two guys who were adding soil to the pitcher's mound and shot me a quizzical look. "We're pretty darn busy right now," the man called Marty said. "What do you need?"

"My name's Archie Goodwin," I told him as we met along the third-base line. "I'm a private investigator with a client whose nephew recently died. Among the dead man's possession were a couple of keys, and we have reason to believe one of them may open gates here at the Polo Grounds."

"That so?" Marty said, clearly uninterested. "So what's this dead guy's moniker?"

"I'm not at liberty to say because of some pending legal actions involving the deceased's estate."

"Whole thing sounds pretty strange to me. I can't see where some keys would be part of an estate," the straw boss said, looking over his shoulder at the crew on the field. "Hey, rake the surface around second base," he snapped, cupping his hand to his mouth. "It's lumpy behind the bag. You can see that clearly from here."

"You're right, it sounds strange," I agreed, "but when lawyers get together, strange things always seem to happen. Maybe these keys have some value as antiques. They look pretty old. Here they are," I said, pulling them out of my pocket. "Recognize either of them?"

"I sure as heck do," Marty said, jerking upright and putting his finger on one. "That's no antique. No question, it's one of our skeleton keys. I can tell by the serial number." He took a key from a chain attached to his belt and held it against the one I had. "Yep, it's one of ours, all right. See how the notches line up perfectly? They're the same, no question. Yours will open every doggone gate around the periphery of this field. All of them."

"What about the other one?"

He peered at it. "Doggoned if it's not from Yankee Stadium. I used to work on their crew a few years back, and their keys are easy to recognize. They're squared off at the top, not round like ours. Say, how did this dead guy happen to have these?" Marty demanded.

"Beats me. Well, thanks for your time, Mr. . . ."

"O'Farrell, Marty O'Farrell. Say, Mr. Goodwin, I'll just take that Polo Grounds key of yours. It belongs to us."

"Sorry," I said, "but it's still part of a probate case, which may go on for some time, lawyers being lawyers, as you know."

"But, we—"

"I promise that when this whole business is done, your key will be returned, and so will the one to your pals on the far side of the Harlem River at the Yankee Stadium." I turned and trotted off before O'Farrell could respond, turning and taking one last look at the crew preparing the field for the arrival of the Pittsburgh Pirates.

Driving back to the brownstone, I was glad O'Farrell, rather than his boss, had been in charge. If the top dog had been present, he might have wondered whether the key in question had played a part in Orson Milbank's shooting. He also might not have given up the fight over that key so easily. But O'Farrell, likely not used to being in charge, was distracted in his attempt to stay on top of the ground crew's work.

It was twelve forty-five when I returned to the

brownstone, which surprised me. My visit to the Polo Grounds had seemed much longer than it was. The good news was that I was back in time for lunch, or so I thought.

I hadn't been back at my desk for more than five minutes when the phone rang. It was Lon Cohen.

"Hi, Archie. I thought you would want to hear the latest about Mona Fentress's campaign for the state senate."

"Of course, we would," I said, indicating to Wolfe that he should pick up his instrument. "Okay, fire away, Lon."

"Our political editor got the word minutes ago from the Fentress office that she has come out one hundred percent behind the Northern Parkway project. And get this: La Fentress is in favor of the original plan, not even the modified version that Orson Milbank had endorsed."

"That is most interesting, Mr. Cohen," Wolfe said. "What do the political analysts on your newspaper conclude about this position of hers?"

"That she realized she had only a slim chance of winning in the fall by opposing the Northern Parkway. Her opponent has been on record as pushing for the road, and all the polls we've seen have indicated that the district's voters are increasingly in favor of it."

"How will the *Gazette* play this development?"

"Right out there on page one, of course. For one thing, we've got a slew of subscribers up in those counties, loyal readers we have had for years. For another, because of the Milbank killing, this is going to be one of the most closely watched elections in years—and not just in this state, but nationally. Every other paper in town will be all over the story, too, along with the wire services, the whole works. Our people will be calling all the predictable sources for comments, including Jonah Keller, Ray Corcoran, the senator's widow, the guy from that conservation group, and Franco Bacelli, of course, if he'll even deign to talk to us."

"Did Mrs. Fentress make a statement?"

"There's just a short quote from her in the press release that a messenger delivered to us and presumably to all the dailies plus the television stations, the radio networks, and the AP, UP, and INS," Lon answered. "She said that 'After much careful consideration and reflection, I have decided that the constituents of this senatorial district would be best served by having the Northern Parkway follow the originally planned route.' That's it. But she's giving a press conference in White Plains at four o'clock this afternoon, and it figures to be a doozy. We're going to be sending two men and a photog."

"Would Mr. Goodwin be allowed to attend this event?" Wolfe asked, swiveling to face me.

"I can't think of any reason why not. I'm not sure they'll even be checking credentials, but I'll have our man Sanders—you've met him, Archie—wait at the door with a *Gazette* press card you can use if it's needed. This circus, and I use the term advisedly, is being held in the auditorium of a school building," Lon said, giving us the address. "Should make for some dandy drama."

"Well, there goes lunch. So, I'm back on my horse and off to the northlands once again," I told Wolfe. "Any instructions?"

"Be alert and observant, of course. But most important, drive with the utmost care," he said. "You have another long voyage ahead."

Wolfe thinks anything more than a trip to his barbershop six blocks away is a major trek. He refuses to ride in a taxi or in a car driven by anyone except me or, on occasion, Saul Panzer.

He also feels anyone else who willingly rides in an automobile takes his life in his own hands. With this in mind, I promised him I would scrupulously obey the speed limits and keep both hands on the wheel at all times.

CHAPTER 22

I located the stately, Gothic-style school building near the center of White Plains with no trouble, arriving almost a half hour before the scheduled four o'clock press conference. Larry Sanders of the *Gazette* greeted me at the front door.

"Nice to see you again, Archie," Sanders said, slipping a press card into my hand. "I hardly think you'll need this, but take it just in case. I got here early, and nobody seems to be checking identi-fication. I think Fentress and her people just want to see a big crowd, which may or may not turn out to her advantage. I've got you a seat with me down front; the place is filling up fast."

Sanders didn't exaggerate. The high-ceilinged hall with rows of cushioned seats sloping down toward a bare stage with only a lectern on it was well over half full, and more people were filing in. I took a seat in the second row and looking around at those nearest me, I recognized several reporters, most of whom I knew by face, a few by name. Kneeling down in front of the first row, a battery of press photographers with flashbulbs in place on their trusty Speed Graphic cameras waited expectantly. This promised to be quite a show.

At the appointed hour, Mona Fentress, regal in a businesslike navy-blue suit and matching pumps, strode confidently onto the stage from the wings amid a smattering of applause and a few hisses. She stood behind the lectern, which had the microphones of the major radio networks attached to it with clamps. Adjusting the main microphone as flashbulbs popped, she looked around the auditorium, moved her glance down to the press contingent, and spotted me, raising her eyebrows and sending the hint of a smile in my direction.

"Thank you all so much for coming here today," she said into the microphone. "I apologize for the short notice, but I felt it was important that I communicate my position both to the press and radio, as well as to the citizens of this district as quickly as possible."

"Your position is that you are a turncoat!" boomed a voice from the back of the auditorium. I swung around to look and saw a uniformed cop lay a beefy hand on the shoulder of a skinny guy about twenty-five.

"That's all right, Officer," Mona Fentress said, holding up a palm. "He can stay, as long as he does not interrupt me again. We are not a nation in which everyone agrees upon everything, nor should we be. The ability to have free and open discussion is the very cornerstone of a democratic society, and I will never interfere with that cornerstone." That brought a mixture of clapping and boos.

"Now, if I may please continue," she said,

adjusting the microphone. "As many here already know, after much soulsearching and conferring with many groups and individuals in this district, I have decided to support and vigorously encourage the construction of the Northern Parkway, using its originally proposed route." More applause and boos.

"The route that I support will reap the maximum benefit for the majority of—" Mona stopped in mid-sentence as a group of fresh-faced young women in sweaters, skirts, and saddle shoes or penny loafers paraded down the center aisle—coeds from Vassar volunteering with Howell Baxter and CLEAN, as I later learned—who held up cardboard signs on sticks that read STOP THE ROAD!, SAVE OUR PARKLANDS!, and PROTECT OUR WAY OF LIFE!

The candidate stood at one side of the podium and watched the procession as it passed by in front of her and marched up a side aisle. None of the sign carriers said a word, but their appearance drew scattered approving "oohs" and "aahs" along with some hisses and shouts of "Girls, go back to the classroom where you belong!" and "This is what happens when we let gals leave home and go off to college without parental supervision!"

Mona Fentress looked on expressionless, then she smiled benevolently. "I respect your rights to protest," she said, "and I am glad to see that all of you did so in a peaceful and respectful manner."

With that, she actually clapped, and I mentally saluted the lady for her grace under pressure.

"But this is really a press conference, first and foremost," she said, "and there are many members of the press here, several of whom I'm sure have questions for me." She looked down at the first several rows.

"Yes, you," she said, pointing to a man who stood.

"I am Dan Morrow, of the *New York Times*, and I would like to ask you how you think Senator Milbank would have felt about you supporting a road that he fought so long and so vigorously against."

"Of course, I recognized you immediately, Mr. Morrow, and I am so glad you are here. Yours is an excellent question. Actually, as you know, the senator had shifted his position somewhat, eventually easing up on his opposition to the parkway. In conversations I had with him shortly before . . . before what happened, I sensed that he might eventually embrace the original route. I cannot be sure of that, of course, but in my heart, I believe Senator Milbank would have taken the position I now have adopted. Yes, you in the blue suit over there."

"Ted Vinson of the White Plains *Reporter Dispatch*," said a young man of no more than twenty-three who got to his feet. "You and your opponent are both in favor of the road being built.

Given that, why should people in this district vote for you instead of him?"

"I will tell you precisely why, Mr. Vinson. Because in my close work with Senator Milbank over the last several years, I have developed a deep knowledge of the needs and wants of the people of all walks of life and all social strata in these three fine counties. My worthy opponent, on the other hand, is a wealthy businessman who has isolated himself from the electorate and has no concept of—or experience with—the struggles everyday citizens go through."

"But never having lived in the district, you can hardly qualify as an expert on our needs yourself," the White Plains reporter persisted.

"However, I do have empathy, I have a caring heart, Mr. Vinson," Mona said, jabbing an index finger at her breast. "And I have a lifelong concern for the underdog. I do not believe the same can be said for my opponent. I also should say at this point that I have had an apartment right here in White Plains for three years, which is my legal address." That drew some applause but also groans of disbelief and a few boos.

"Yes, you next," Mona said, nodding and pointing to the man sitting next to me, who had risen.

"Larry Sanders of the *Gazette*. Mrs. Fentress, how do you think that Franco Bacelli will react to your stance on the road?"

That sent the crowd to buzzing, along with some shouts, including "Yeah, just how you gonna handle him?" and "You could find yourself in big trouble, lady."

Mona brushed a strand of hair from her forehead and cleared her throat. "Mr. Sanders, unless I am very much mistaken, Mr. Bacelli is but one citizen among the tens of thousands who reside in this district. And while I will solicit and respect the opinions of each and every person who dwells in this constituency, I cannot let myself be swayed by any single individual and his or her special interests, concerns, or desires. I must consider the needs and wishes of the majority. To do any less would be a dereliction of duty on the part of any public servant, Mr. Sanders." That brought well over half of the crowd to its feet, clapping and cheering.

The rest of the session, which continued for over an hour, was pretty much more of the same, with reporters from papers both in New York City and the senatorial district peppering Mona Fentress with questions about her experience, her familiarity with the region, and her concern about what impact the new road would have on the local economy and the environment. Bacelli's name was not mentioned again in the questions.

Overall, I felt she handled herself well, and when she finally called an end to the questioning, she told the audience that she would hold more sessions like this one. "Except," she said, "they will be more like town meetings than press conferences, because I am most interested in what the citizens of this district want and need from their elected representatives."

As the auditorium emptied out, I hung around as several reporters and a couple of other people, presumably voters, talked to Mona. A square-jawed guy about my age with a sandy crew cut stood at her side the entire time, smiling and nodding his approval of everything she said. After the last person had drifted away, Mona waved me over.

"Archie Goodwin! How nice of you to come and watch me get grilled by the press and the voting public. How do you think I did?"

"I hardly qualify as an expert on the rough and tumble world of politics, but I would say you more than held your own. You took a few good punches, but I don't see any scars or bruises."

"I really appreciate those words. Archie, I'd like you to meet my campaign manager, Doug Yardley."

"Nice to meet you, Mr. Goodwin," he said with a grin as he pumped my hand. "Mona has said a lot about you, all of it good."

"Glad to hear that. How do you feel your candidate did today?"

"I thought she was absolutely terrific, especially when those Vassar girls walked down the aisle with the signs, and also her answer to the question about Bacelli. We were hoping someone would bring that up."

"I can't take the credit. That was really Doug's doing," she said. "He told me beforehand that we would likely get a question about Bacelli and also get some sort of demonstration from the people at CLEAN, and that I should be very welcoming to them."

"It tends to take a little of the wind out of their sails when you applaud something your opponents do," Yardley said. "I should head back to the office now," he told Mona. "See you there in the morning, okay?"

"Bye, Doug. I'll be in the office tomorrow around eight thirty. Archie, can I talk you into buying me a drink?"

"Why not? Do you have a car?"

"It's parked over at our new campaign office, which is just a block away from here. You can drop me there later. I know a nice, quiet little lounge where we can talk."

CHAPTER 23

I drove us to the lounge, with Mona chattering excitedly all the way about her campaign. The press conference or rally, or whatever you want to call it, had really gotten her charged up, and she wanted to go back over every minute of it. I probably said no more than ten words during the ride.

The bar was indeed quiet, as well as dark, with its only customers being two old gents sitting several stools apart at the bar. We settled into an upholstered booth in the corner, and then I got drinks from the bartender—a bourbon on the rocks for her and a Coke for me.

"Not drinking?" she asked as I rejoined her.

"I will definitely have something when I get home, after I've put the car to bed for the night."

"You are most virtuous, Archie Goodwin," she said, clinking her glass against mine. "Mark me down as impressed."

"Don't be. On more than a couple of occasions, I've driven with a drink or two in me, and I could feel it. I like to know that I am totally in control when I'm behind the wheel. Tell me about your campaign manager."

"Doug? He's a great guy, really knows his stuff. He's worked on a lot of campaigns for state legislators, and even helped get a client elected to the US House of Representatives from a district up around Syracuse in what was considered a big upset at the time. That's when I first heard about him."

"Is Yardley's experience the reason you didn't go with Ross Davies to shepherd your campaign?"

Mona looked down and stirred her drink. "No, there was another reason, Archie," she said after a pause of several seconds. "Ross was dead-set against the Northern Parkway. He felt it would destroy what he called the 'bucolic environment' of these counties, particularly the northern two."

"Yeah, Westchester, nice as it is, hardly qualifies as totally bucolic. There's a bunch of good-size towns here, including the one we're in right now. But both Putnam and Dutchess certainly can be called rural, at least for the present."

"Well, anyway, Ross was even opposed to Orson's compromise proposal, although he kept quiet about it. He didn't want to see any road built. He and I would have locked horns from day one. It would have become an impossible situation. I suspect Ross realized that, too."

"Were you in favor of the road when you worked for Milbank?"

"I didn't share his strong aversion to it, but after all, he was my boss, and I respected him, so I held my own counsel. Have you and Nero Wolfe gotten anywhere in figuring out who the killer was?"

"Not yet, I'm sorry to say."

"And I'm sure the police continue to be in the dark."

"If they've gotten anywhere, they certainly are not sharing it with us. Other than today's meeting, what kind of reaction have you received about your position on the road?"

"A congratulatory phone call from Jonah Keller, which was to be expected, and a telegram cheering me on from Ray Corcoran, also no surprise."

"Any negative calls?"

She chuckled. "Howell Baxter of CLEAN called our office to say that he would use every means at his disposal to fight me, but he didn't specify just what those means would be."

"Other than having a group of rosy-cheeked, skirted young women march through the auditorium holding signs?"

"They are all students from Vassar, as you probably know. Howell has got a big following on the campus. I'm just glad many of them are still too young to vote," she said, laughing.

"Other than Baxter, have you received any threats—I mean threats of a perilous nature?"

She bit her lower lip and nodded. "Two telephone calls this morning, about a half hour apart, anonymous, of course. A different man's voice each time, but the message was essentially the same: 'The same thing could happen to you that happened to Orson Milbank.'"

"Any thoughts on who's behind the calls?"

She sniffed. "Our old friend Bacelli, without doubt."

"I don't know, Mona. He's gone out of his way to say he had nothing to do with Milbank's killing."

"Huh! And you, Archie Goodwin, cynical, hard-bitten veteran New York private investigator, actually believe him?"

"I'll plead guilty to the cynical part, some of the time anyway. But I've never thought of myself as being hard-bitten."

"Oh, maybe not," she conceded. "But I hardly see you as someone who would accept anything Franco Bacelli says at face value."

"Good point. Are you taking precautions against this threat, regardless of who might have made it?"

"I haven't, other than to report it to the various local police departments in this district. What can I do, hire a bunch of bodyguards? Hardly practical, given that over the next several weeks, I'm going to be standing in front of what I hope will be large crowds many times, where anybody can easily take a potshot at me. A dozen bodyguards wouldn't be able to prevent that from happening any more than they could have prevented Orson's shooting in front of several thousand baseball fans in the nation's largest city."

"You paint a pretty grim picture," I said.

"I suppose, but then I went into this campaign with my eyes open, Archie. Call me a realist. I am damned if I'm going to let this thug or anybody else intimidate me. If we all were to let that happen, nobody would ever end up running for office."

"I can't quarrel with that position, but you still need to be careful, Mona. Don't confuse being intrepid with being reckless. By the way, I'm repeating a question I asked you some time back. How is your husband reacting to your new role as a campaigner?"

"Charles? He thinks that I am absolutely crazy, of course, even more so since I came out in favor of the road," she said, waving her husband away with a manicured hand. "And he also acts upset that I'm moving into an apartment here in White Plains. That's just a pose on his part, though. He's as easy to see through as a plate-glass display window at Macy's Herald Square. He really wants me out of the way so he can be free to spend more time with the glamorous and charming Caroline Jackson Willis, she of the society pages, the benefit luncheons and dances, and the numerous save-the-world committees."

"This from one who is very glamorous and charming herself," I said. "Speaking of your relationship with Mr. Fentress the advertising man, are you worried that voters are going to wonder why you and your husband live apart?"

"It did not seem to hurt Orson that he and Elise spent so much time apart," she said with a toss of her blonde mane. "I'm hoping the voters will give me the same leeway they gave him."

"Unfortunately for you, though, most people tend to cut men more slack than women when it comes to situations relating to propriety."

She nodded, pursing her lips. "Your point is well taken, I'm sad to admit. The world is not always fair, I know that all too well, Archie. But I am absolutely convinced that we're going to be seeing a lot more women in public life in the years ahead. Although I don't place myself in the same league as Senator Margaret Chase Smith, I like to think of myself as something of a trailblazer. Do you think of that as arrogance on my part?"

"No, I don't, not in the least. Given the way the men in this great country's government have bollixed things up, more women holding office can only be seen as a good thing," I said, raising my Coke glass in salute to the lady.

CHAPTER 24

It was seven forty-five when I got back to the brownstone, which meant Nero Wolfe was in the dining room consuming Fritz's breaded pork tenderloin. I had already said I would not be at dinner tonight because of, one, my trip to White Plains and, two, a soiree I had been invited to at Lily Rowan's apartment on East Sixty-Third Street between Park and Madison.

Calling Lily's splendid abode an "apartment" hardly does it justice. It actually is a duplex penthouse perched atop a ten-story building and furnished with, among other things, a nineteen-by-thirty-three-foot Kashan carpet, an off-white Bösendorfer Imperial grand piano with ninety-seven keys (I've counted them), and artwork by Renoir, Monet, and Matisse. If you're wondering where her money came from, and there's plenty of it, she is the only offspring of an Irish immigrant who made millions heading up a company that built much of Manhattan's sewer system in the early years of the century. Those millions are now Lily's.

This is a good time to mention that although Lily is one of the wealthiest women in Manhattan, that wealth is not and never has been what I find most attractive about her. I could give you at least a dozen better reasons for my wanting to spend time in the presence of the lady. And let it be known that when we go out on the town, whether it be to dinner at Rusterman's or other fine restaurants, dancing at the Churchill, or to a Rangers game at the Garden, I pick up the tab. Period.

With all her piles of dough, she might well be described as a lady of leisure, although to her credit she serves on the committees of more charitable groups than I can keep track of, and she always seems to be throwing open her doors to host parties that benefit these groups. Tonight was one such event: a gathering to raise funds for an orphanage badly in need of an additional wing.

After sprucing myself up and changing, I grabbed a cab and arrived at Lily's at twenty minutes after eight. "Escamillo!" she said as she opened the door, "I thought you had forgotten all about this evening."

"Forgotten about one of your memorable bashes? Unthinkable, absolutely unthinkable," I said in mock horror, encircling her slender waist with my arm and planting a prolonged smooch on her lips.

"Whatever will people think?" she said, looking over her shoulder at the crowd that milled about with cocktails and canapés in her sprawling living room and adjoining parlor while a string trio played Mozart in an alcove.

"I believe we were barely noticed in that little embrace," I answered. "Everybody appears to be more involved in talking and drinking up your pricey liquor and gobbling down your shrimp and caviar and the numerous other delectables you have so generously set out for them."

"All for a very good cause, my fine man," she purred, taking my arm and leading me to one corner of the room, where a red-jacketed bartender poured drinks of generous proportion.

Fortified with a single-malt scotch, I allowed Lily to steer me around the room, introducing me to a variety of her guests, all of whom looked like they were totally at home in their opulent surroundings. After making the circuit, Lily suggested we step out onto the terrace.

"Ah, perchance have you lured me out here to neck?" I demanded.

"Banish the thought—at least for now," she replied, jabbing me in the ribs with a slim finger. "I just wanted you to myself for a few minutes, away from the madding crowd."

"They don't seem all that madding to me, but I like your idea, especially on a night like this," I said as a summer breeze wafted over us. "I like to view the city from up here above it all. Makes me feel important, even though I know better. Say, I have a question for you, oh, lovely one."

"Well, for heaven's sake, Escamillo, don't hold back. You never have before. Out with it. By the way, you're important to me, damned important, and don't you ever forget it."

"Thanks for that, my love. Do you by chance happen to know Caroline Jackson Willis?"

Lily put her hands on her hips. "What is it about you and attractive women, Mr. Goodwin? First you pry information out of me concerning Elise DuVal, and now you want to know about another exotic and shapely female. Does this have anything to do with the investigation into Orson Milbank's death, or are you interested for other, more lascivious reasons?"

"Lascivious, eh? Now it is my turn to say 'banish the thought.'" I parried. "First off, I have never laid eyes on Mrs. Willis, so I did not know she was attractive, let alone exotic and shapely. Second, I doubt very much that she has any connection with the Milbank case, except indirectly. It seems she has drawn the interest of one Charles Fentress, advertising executive and husband of the woman who is now running for Milbank's senate seat."

Lily smirked. "I would reverse that, my dear, and phrase it that Fentress has drawn the interest of said lady—and I use that term loosely."

"I thought you told me you did not like to be viewed as catty."

"For certain persons, I will make an exception, and Caroline Jackson Willis happens to be one of those persons."

"Are you suggesting that she, dare I say it, is a man hunter?"

"Very good!" she chirped, clapping twice. "I wouldn't tell this to just anybody, but when she goes out after a man, she usually gets him. Her husbands, Edgar Jackson and Lance Willis, both were very rich and very married when she met them. Then they each got divorced to marry her."

"Let me guess what comes next: she divorced them, and neither man is as rich as he once was."

"See what happens when you hang around me long enough, Escamillo? You start thinking like I do."

"I'll have to reflect on whether that's a good thing. What can you tell me about this lady and Mr. Fentress?"

"Not a lot, I'm afraid. Oh, I've heard more than a few rumors. But if they have become an item as you suggest, they've been very discreet about it. I have never seen them together in public—not once. In the last few weeks, I've been at three gatherings like this one tonight that Caroline has also attended, and each time, she was alone. That's somewhat rare for her; she usually has a man in tow. Maybe she's trying to keep him to herself. My suspicion is that when they *are* together, it is usually at intimate dinner parties in private homes, three or four couples, that sort of thing."

"Is the lady in question by chance here this evening?" I asked, looking around the room.

"No, this is not one of her good works. Be thankful, because if she had been present, she probably would have latched on to you like a barnacle by now and ended up trying to monopolize you."

"That would have been very hard for her to do, what with me trying to monopolize you."

"Have I ever told you that you are a silver-tongued rascal? Where did you hear that they were seeing each other?"

"From a newspaperman."

"Your old friend and poker-playing adversary Lon Cohen, no doubt. Well, through his paper's intrepid columnists, he probably has far better pipelines to dalliances among the so-called upper crust than I do."

"Dalliances, is that what they're called? I can't imagine that anyone's got a better pipeline than you."

"You say the sweetest things to a girl. As nice as the evening is out here, we should go back in. I don't want my guests to feel that I've been ignoring them."

"Heaven forbid. There must be at least ten men in this penthouse right now who wish they were in my shoes at this moment."

"Now *that* really is sweet. After this humble little gathering has ended and everyone else has gone, would you like to be a dear and stay around to help me clean up?"

"I thought you would never ask," I said as we strolled back indoors and into the rarefied world of Manhattan society.

CHAPTER 25

The next morning after breakfast, I had barely settled into my chair in the office when the phone rang. I answered with my usual, "Nero Wolfe's office, Archie Goodwin speaking."

"Archie, why haven't I heard anything from you?" It was the plaintive voice of Elise DuVal. "You said you would keep me posted regularly, but I feel like I have been cast in the role of the neglected client, sitting by a telephone that doesn't ring."

"I'm sorry, Elise. It is just that we simply don't have anything to report, but I confess I am at fault for not keeping in better touch with you. Am I forgiven?"

"Oh, of course, you are. And just what do you think of that goody-two-shoes who has decided to run for Orson's seat?" she continued as her tone hardened. "Do you find that as disgusting as I do?"

"I wouldn't have put it quite that way myself, but I'm interested in why you think so."

"Oh, Archie, isn't it obvious, for God's sake? That woman has ambition oozing from every pore and always had. Remember, I'm an actress, or at least I was. Of all people, I know ambition when I see it. From the day she joined Orson's staff, she wanted his job, wanted to be a senator herself."

"You didn't mention that to me before."

"I didn't think I had to. I figured that you would realize it once you learned more about her. You are right about one thing, though. At first, I didn't even consider her to be a suspect. But then, when she announced she was running for Orson's seat, things started adding up."

"Go on. I want to hear more."

"Whoever shot Orson, you can bet Mona Fentress hired the gunman, either herself or through some go-between."

"Yet when we first talked, you said any one of three people might have killed your husband: Franco Bacelli, Jonah Keller, and Ray Corcoran. You never once suggested Mrs. Fentress as a suspect."

"That was then and this is now. The scales have now fallen from my eyes. That woman only waited barely over a week after his death to announce that she was running."

"What about the rumor that she and your husband were having an affair?"

"Now I see that for exactly what it was," Elise said. "A clever piece of acting on her part—and I know acting when I see it, although the closest I'll ever come to an Oscar is seeing a picture of one of the statues in the newspapers the day after the show. Mona wanted people to think she and

Orson were carrying on because that would make her seem the least likely suspect, right?"

"Maybe. But if she knew he was going to get shot at the ball park, she must have nerves of steel, because she was standing right next to him," I said.

"I believe she does have nerves of steel, Archie. Ever since the shooting and even before she announced she was going to run, have you noticed which of us, Mona or me, has had their picture in the paper more often? Not the grieving widow, but the faithful aide to the senator, who had to witness his death from up close. She's milked that for everything she can, and she continues to milk it."

"So as you now see it, Mona Fentress ranks even ahead of Franco Bacelli as the prime suspect in the shooting?"

"Yes, that is how I now see it."

"All right, I will inform Mr. Wolfe of everything you've said, and I promise we will do a better job of keeping you informed."

"Thank you, Archie," she said in a tired voice. "Just remember two words: Mona Fentress."

I sat for several minutes, digesting Elise DuVal's comments. If Mona Fentress had indeed orchestrated Milbank's shooting, she would have needed help, some sort of go-between, as Elise suggested. Someone who could enlist a sharp-shooter like the late Dick Thompson. On a hunch, I called Lon Cohen.

"Rare is the day I don't hear from you," he said. "What favor do you now seek? And make it fast, because we're on a deadline."

"As long as I've known you, you've always been on a deadline. How often can you use that excuse?"

"As often as I can get away with it. What gives?"

"The *Gazette* threw a big bash at the Waldorf Astoria for honored war veterans last year, right?"

"Sure, that was our 'Heroes Among Us' banquet—and I was there, sitting at the publisher's table. For my money, it was a first-class event, one of the best things the *Gazette* has ever done in the way of community service. At the table with us were two Medal of Honor winners plus a guy with the Navy Cross and another one who wore the Silver Star. These are the real heroes, all right, not a bunch of egotistical, overweight, and overpaid baseball players who never seem to have time to sign a kid's autograph book."

"Nice speech, Lon. It almost makes me want to stand and applaud. Now, I have a favor to ask."

"Why am I not surprised?"

"I don't think what I'm about to ask will be all that difficult. I assume somewhere in your vast building there is a guest list from the heroes' banquet."

"Probably. Does this have anything to do with that marine whose obit we talked about?"

"Yes, in part, it does."

"Care to tell me any more?"

"Not at the moment, but as Mr. Wolfe assured you earlier, if and when something breaks, you and the *Gazette* will be the first to know, as has almost always been the case in the past where we are involved. And remember, we did tell the identity of our client as an act of good faith."

"True enough. All right, I'll check with our special events people about the list and get back to you." He did, less than a half hour later, and after leaving a note for Wolfe and telling Fritz I'd be out for a while, I stepped into the June sun and took a ten-block walk to the *Gazette* building.

When I walked into Lon's office, he was on the phone as usual and waved me to a chair. "Yeah, yeah, I know," he barked into the mouthpiece, "but we've already run two major pieces on that new bridge. Can't that man find something else to write about? Tell him to show a little initiative for a change."

Lon slammed the phone down and turned to me, shaking his head. "For more than a year, this guy begged to be made an around-the-town columnist, and the managing editor finally gave in. But it turns out this bozo hasn't had an original idea in his life, and everything he suggests has been done to death, by us and by every other paper in town. By far the most interesting damned city on the planet, well over seven million of us according to the folks who take the census, and he can't seem to find anything new. If he doesn't start showing some imagination, it will be right back to the police beat for him."

"The life of a big-time newspaper executive sure isn't all that it's cracked up to be," I said.

"It's sure as shooting isn't, Archie. Oh, here's what you asked for." He handed me a thick bundle of typewritten pages, held together by twine. "Everybody's on here."

"Not just the veterans, but all the others who attended the banquet as well?"

"Oh, don't worry, they are here as well. This was an expensive evening, and we got a lot of businesses and associations to help us sponsor it. Every one of them that kicked in money or food got invited. Archie, this should have occurred to me earlier: there's a good chance that Richard Thompson was at the dinner."

"More than a good chance, Lon. I happen to know that he was there. And for the record, he also was the subject of one of the features in your paper's 'Heroes Among Us' series a while back."

"Jeez, you'd think I would have remembered that, or at least checked on it once you and Wolfe pointed me toward the guy," Lon said, slapping his forehead with a palm. "I sit before you a chagrined man. I must be slipping if I don't even have a handle on what my own paper has done."

"Your secret is safe with me, newshound.

Besides, you've got a lot of balls to juggle in your job. Now, by chance, do you have a seating chart to the Waldorf event?"

"No, although I anticipated your question and asked," Lon said. "There was open seating, although we encouraged the sponsors to spread out so there was one or more of them at every table to interact with the veterans. So nobody here knows exactly who sat where."

"Thanks, I appreciate it," I said, rising to leave.

"Just bring that list back when you're done with it. Our people have only one other copy."

I got back to the brownstone at just after ten, meaning Wolfe would not be down from the plant rooms for almost an hour. That gave me time to wade through the dozens of pages of attendees. Going over the list, I occasionally made a light pencil mark next to one of the names. Every individual I had expected to find was listed, giving me a sense of satisfaction.

I had just finished with the final page of names as the elevator came to life, indicating Wolfe had begun his descent. I placed the stack of sheets on his desk blotter and turned to the orchid germination records Theodore had put on my desk earlier that morning so I could enter them into the files.

"Good morning, Archie. Did you sleep well?" Wolfe asked as he invariably does when he enters the office in the morning. I gave him an affirmative answer as he placed a raceme of orchids in the vase on his desk, settled into his chair, and rang for beer.

"What is this?" he demanded as he held up the sheaf of papers.

"Do you recall my mentioning that Marguerite Hackman told me her brother had attended a dinner at the Waldorf Astoria for decorated war veterans from the New York area last year?"

"I do," he snapped.

"What you have there is a list of all those, veterans and others, who attended that dinner. I felt you would find it of interest. I put light pencil marks beside some of the names."

He frowned but began reading. I turned back to the germination records, listening to the faint rustle of paper each time he flipped a page. It took him far less time than me to go through the roster, perhaps twenty minutes, and when he finished, he exhaled loudly. "Very satisfactory."

Those two words from Wolfe are the equivalent of an ordinary mortal screaming "Spectacular!" or "Magnificent!" I swiveled to face him, stifling a grin. "Glad you think so," I told him.

"Your notebook please," he said, finally taking a sip from the beer that had gone untouched during his perusal of the pages.

CHAPTER 26

The first task Wolfe gave me was not one I relished, but I had been expecting it and knew that at some point, it had to be done. That point had arrived. I dialed the Flushing number and got an answer on the second ring.

"Hello, Mrs. Hackman. This is the man who called himself Alan Nelson when we met at your house."

"Of course, I recognize your voice," she said in a tone that strongly suggested she would rather be doing ironing or vacuuming than talking to me. "What is it that you want?"

"I would like to come and see you again, this time as myself."

"And just who would that be?"

"My name is Archie Goodwin. I am a private investigator in Manhattan, and I work for another detective, Nero Wolfe."

"Now *his* name, I recognize. Tell me why I should bother seeing you, Mr. Goodwin?"

"It involves your brother and the shooting death of State Senator Orson Milbank at the Polo Grounds."

I heard nothing other than breathing on the other end for several seconds. "You are not going to bring me good news, are you?"

"I'm afraid not, Mrs. Hackman. After my visit the other night, you have every right to demand total honesty from me, plus an apology."

"I will consider accepting that apology, but you still have not told me why I should see you."

"This is not something I prefer to discuss on the telephone. I will say only that Mr. Wolfe and I are interested in identifying the individual who we believe helped to destroy your brother's life, and we feel there's a good chance you can aid us with that identification."

Another pause. "Just when do you propose coming here, Mr. Goodwin?"

"Whenever it is convenient for you. Given my history with you, I realize I am in no position to make demands. What about this afternoon?"

"All right, three o'clock," she said, her voice now several degrees warmer than when she answered the phone, but still by no means friendly. "This time, I would like to see identification with a photograph, if you happen to have some."

"You will see it before you unlock your door," I said.

The second taxi ride I had taken to Flushing in the last few days got me to Marguerite Hackman's house precisely at three. I rang the bell and held up my private investigator's license, with its mug shot, so that Marguerite could see it through the glass in her front door. After nodding, she swung the door open for me. Her expression now was every bit as sad as her voice had been when we first met, and I knew I was in large measure responsible.

"Thank you for agreeing to see me," I said as I stepped into the living room.

"Your apology is accepted," she said, still unsmiling. "Please sit down. Would you like some coffee?"

I told her no, thanks, and parked myself in an easy chair while she dropped onto the sofa, eying me with an expectant expression. When I hesitated, collecting my thoughts, she spoke: "Mr. Goodwin, my brother is dead and nothing in God's world can bring him back. You need not worry about sparing my feelings at this point. I have no more capacity for mourning. Please feel free to say what you have to."

"Nero Wolfe has been hired to find out who killed Senator Orson Milbank, and—"

"Isn't that a job for the police department?"

"Yes, it is, but the individual who hired Mr. Wolfe does not feel they have been doing a good job."

"Well, I do read the newspapers regularly, and over the years I have seen Nero Wolfe's name appear on a few occasions, usually to do with the solving of a crime, if I'm not mistaken. If your name was in any of those stories as well, I'm sorry but I don't remember it."

"Don't be sorry. Mr. Wolfe is the one who does all the solving. I'm just his errand boy."

That almost brought a smile, but not quite. "Mrs. Hackman," I continued, "you said not to spare your feelings. All right, here goes: it seems probable, although not provable at present, that your brother fired the shot that killed the senator, very likely with the same rifle that I saw in the closet upstairs when I was here before. Is it still there?"

"Yes, yes, it is," she said. "Are those keys you took when you were here before somehow connected to all of this?"

"You are very perceptive," I told her. "One was a key that opens all sorts of gates at the Polo Grounds; the other does much the same at Yankee Stadium. You had told me those were among the places he briefly worked. Any idea why he would take keys away with him after he had left those jobs? Revenge against the Giants and Yankees for having fired him, perhaps?"

"Maybe, but I don't think so," Marguerite said, her expression thoughtful. "When Dick was a kid, before he got all wild and rebellious, he loved baseball, absolutely adored it, particularly the Yankees and Giants, but never the Dodgers, for some reason. Anyway, he got hold of everything he could find about the two teams. Those baseball trading cards boys like to collect so much, of course, but also autographed pictures of the players that he had sent away for."

"Did he go to games often?"

She shook her head. "It was the Depression, and we didn't have much money. My father took Dick a few times, to see Babe Ruth and Lou Gehrig and Mel Ott, but not often. Later, I think he used to sneak into games. He never said so, but I'm sure of it."

"Not surprising," I said. "Kids have been doing that for years, at every level from the bush leagues on up to the big time. I found ways to get into games for nothing myself back in my home county in Ohio. Back to those keys, Mrs. Hackman. Why would he take them?"

"Dick may possibly have been angry about losing those jobs with the Giants and Yankees, although during that period about a year or two ago, he was more irrational than angry most of the time, as indeed he was right up to . . . up to his death. I really think he took the keys as souvenirs. It certainly wouldn't have been with the intent to get into the Polo Grounds to shoot that senator. That whole business came along much later."

"You may be right," I said. "Back to what I told you when I came in. It's all but a sure thing that your brother shot the senator."

Marguerite nodded. "Since your last visit, I have done a great deal of thinking and reflecting on events, and I have come to the same conclusion," she said quietly. "As I told you, Dick was a very troubled man."

"It sounds like he had good reason to be, what with all he had seen and been through during the war. Your brother may have fired the fatal shot, but it's more than likely that he was a pawn, not the planner of the crime. That is the person Mr. Wolfe seeks. And to do that, we need your help."

"By that, I assume you mean my trying to identify the man who called here several times and visited Dick once."

"Yes. But first, are you absolutely sure it was a man?"

"I don't know how sure I am about any of this any longer, Mr. Goodwin. The voice on the telephone certainly seemed to be a masculine one, although I suppose voices can be disguised."

"Do you think you would recognize that voice if you heard it again?"

"I honestly believe I would, yes. I'm pretty good that way. When I listen to those radio shows that have movie stars on as guests, I can almost always identify the actor or actress before someone says their name."

"What about the figure you saw from your bedroom window, the person who came to the house to visit your brother?"

"Now that really could have been almost anyone. It was dark outside, and I'm assuming that it was a man. He had a hat pulled down low over his face, as I believe I mentioned to you when you were here before."

"Might that individual have been a woman?"

"I suppose anything is possible. I'm not sure how large the figure I saw was. It may have been a woman dressed like a man. I feel like I'm on the witness stand," Marguerite said, running a nervous hand through her dusty blonde hair.

"Sorry, I didn't mean to act like a lawyer or a district attorney grilling you, Mrs. Hackman. It's just that we are fairly short of information about this person, and you have actually talked to him—if we can assume it's a man."

"I really think that I've told you everything I can. I don't see that there's any more I can do."

"Mr. Wolfe believes you can be of help, if you are willing."

"Is it anything . . . illegal?"

"Absolutely not."

"All right, tell me what would be expected, and I will make a decision," she said firmly. "But hear me on this: I will not be pushed into something that I do not want to do."

"I understand," I told her, proceeding to lay out the plan Wolfe had devised. She listened, sometimes nodding, sometimes frowning.

Forty-five minutes later, I left Marguerite Hackman's house. She had finally talked me into having some coffee, and she also insisted on calling a taxi to pick me up. "They're so difficult to find in this neighborhood," she said.

"Sometimes, I feel like we here are a forgotten part of New York."

"That may be, but it is not a part of the city I will soon forget," I told her as I stepped out of her house and strode to the yellow cab idling at the curb.

CHAPTER 27

When I got home, Wolfe had finished his afternoon session with the orchids and was reading *Modern Arms and Free Men* by Vannevar Bush. I reported on my meeting with Mrs. Hackman, and although I did not get a "very satisfactory" this time, Wolfe approved of its outcome.

My next task was easily as challenging as my assignment in Flushing. Wolfe presented me with a sheet on which he had written a list of those he wanted me to round up and invite to the brownstone the next night. As invariably happens when the man I work for thinks he has zeroed in on the target of an investigation, he invites all of the principals of the case to his office for what Inspector Cramer calls "one of those damned charades of his." Never mind that those so-called charades invariably present Cramer with the solution to a crime and the individual responsible for it.

Over the years, the amazing thing to me has been that I can usually, albeit sometimes with cajoling, get every one of the suspects in a case to show up on our doorstep, even the guilty party or parties. "Hubris invariably overcomes the fear of detection," Wolfe has said as an explanation as to why the culprit shows up, only to be led away by the police.

As I looked over the list I had been given, I hoped hubris would once again be at work in the mind of one or more among these people. Wolfe obviously knew who it was, or he wouldn't be having this party. The best I had been able to do was narrow it down to two, or maybe three.

My first call was to Elise DuVal. "Do you mean that Nero Wolfe has found the killer?" she said in the breathless tone she may have perfected years before in front of Hollywood cameras.

"It appears that way, although he hasn't shared a name with me, so we will both be surprised tomorrow night."

"Wait a minute, Archie. After all, I am the client. Shouldn't I know who it is right now?"

"Sorry, but it does not work that way with Nero Wolfe. All of us are going to learn at the same time."

"Just who do you mean by 'all of us'?"

"You will find that out when you get here tomorrow night."

"That simply is not fair! After all, I'm the one spending the money on this."

"Elise, I believe that when all of this is finished, you will be satisfied that you got your money's worth—and more—from Nero Wolfe."

"Well, I still don't like it," she said petulantly. "Can't you at least give me a little hint?"

I laughed. "No, and for a very good reason. I don't even know myself which donkey—or maybe donkeys—Mr. Wolfe is going to pin the tail on."

That got a laugh out of her. "All right, Archie. But you have to promise to take me to dinner after this is all over."

"What do you think your neighbor Lily Rowan will think of that?"

"Oh, Lily's a good sport. Besides, I'll tell her it was my idea, not yours."

"And that will make it all right?"

"Of course, it will, Archie. She has nothing whatever to fear from me."

"It's not you that Lily will worry about, but what the hell. That dinner will be on me."

"You are a doll. I've thought so since I met you. I'll see you tomorrow night at nine."

Several of the others on the list were a harder sell. I got hold of Mona Fentress, and she definitely did not fancy the idea of a gathering at Wolfe's, nor did I think her husband would.

"Archie, I'm so terribly busy with my campaign right now," she argued. "I have appearances every day, every night, which is essential, because I'm playing catch-up with my so-called esteemed opponent, who has a big head start. I had planned to be meeting people and passing out leaflets all day tomorrow up in Chappaqua, Mount Kisco, and Pound Ridge. Besides, Charles won't like the idea of coming, either, I can tell you that now."

"If you both do not come, you will be conspicuous by your absence, and that could be a far bigger detriment to your campaign. And after all, you can still campaign during the day."

"I do not like it, Archie, not one bit."

"You don't like murder, either, do you? I have the utmost confidence that you can persuade your husband to join you here tonight, nine o'clock sharp."

"Who else will be present?"

"A number of interested parties. I expect to hear back from you in the next half hour telling me both of you will be present. How would it look if the late senator's trusted aide and her husband were so uninterested in finding his killer that they couldn't be bothered to attend a gathering investigating the murder?"

"But it is a private investigation, not an official one. And really, just what is it going to prove?"

"That remains to be seen. Also, it is entirely possible members of the police department will be present."

"That seems most unorthodox."

"Nero Wolfe is unorthodox by his very nature."

"Well . . . I will talk to Charles. But I can't guarantee anything."

"Oh, I believe you can, Mona," I said. "I'm placing my bets on you and your powers of persuasion. Remember, I have seen you in action in front of a heavily hostile crowd. I believe you to be capable of great things."

Jonah Keller was even more intractable than Mrs. Fentress. "What the hell, Goodwin, why should I bother coming down to some private eye's place in Manhattan just to hear him pontificate? I know all about Nero Wolfe and his bluster."

Talk about the pot calling the kettle black, I thought. But what I said was, "I would think you'd want to be present to defend your position."

"What position? What are you talking about?"

"Your position as a staunch defender of the Northern Parkway and an equally staunch opponent of the late and very much mourned Orson D. Milbank. If you are absent from this gathering, people are sure to wonder why. A sign of some guilt, perhaps?"

Several of the next dozen words out of Keller's mouth are among those the *Gazette* or any other newspaper will not allow into its columns. I waited until he had wound down like a tired alarm clock. "Nine o'clock tomorrow night," I said, giving him the address.

More words spewed forth from his mouth, but I could tell that he had fired his best shot and found himself out of ammunition. I put a check mark next to his name as one who would be attending. Ray Corcoran was an easier sell. "Oh yes, Archie Goodwin," he said smoothly. "So you say Mr. Wolfe will inform us as to the status of the Milbank murder investigation? I, for one, am interested in what he has to say. Sure, mark me down as accepting. I will be there. Sounds like a most interesting evening."

Next I called Howell Baxter of CLEAN. "Archie Goodwin, that Ohio-lad-turned-city-boy who favored me with a visit," he cackled. "Now just what can I do for you, son?"

I told him about tomorrow night's gathering, and he laughed heartily. "You really want me to come down to New York and listen to your boss show off about how smart he is? Sorry, but you got yourself the wrong fella. I make it a point to keep my distance from that big city of yours. Haven't been there in several years, and I see no reason to go there now."

"Well, that is surely too bad, Mr. Baxter," I told him. "This would have been a fine chance for you to be in the same room with such people as Jonah Keller and Ray Corcoran. On an equal footing with them, you might say. And it is quite possible this meeting will get some press coverage."

"Say, I've got a group of nice young ladies from Vassar who could come along with me. They've just made some new signs that—"

"No, Mr. Baxter, stop right there. I've seen those sign-carrying girls of yours, and they are absolutely adorable, as well as effective. But for this meeting, Mr. Wolfe has requested only you.

We want you to be on the same stage, so to speak, as Mr. Keller and Mr. Corcoran. Unless, of course, you would feel uncomfortable being in the same room with them."

"Uncomfortable with those two jackasses? Hell, I could out-argue both of them at once. Together, they haven't got a brain worth talking about. All right, dammit, I'll be there. Give me the address."

Immediately after I hung up with Baxter, the phone rang. "You win, Archie, we will come," Mona Fentress said. "I don't like it, and I can assure you that Charles likes it even less, but if this will help in finding Orson's killer, the time spent is more than worth it."

I thanked her and then tackled the three men who had worked on Milbank's team. Ross Davies and Todd Armstrong both readily agreed to come, while Keith Musgrove balked. "I really don't see what could be served by my attending such a function," he said in that high-pitched voice that grated on me.

"I know how close to the senator you were," I said. "You must be interested in hearing how the investigation into his death is progressing."

"But as you have described it, this is not a formal inquiry," he argued. "What can possibly come of it? The whole business sounds like a total waste of time."

"Mrs. Fentress said she will come," I replied. "And, by the way, so will Messrs. Davies and

Armstrong. So the late senator's whole team will be on hand. Except you, of course, if you choose for whatever reason to stay away. Your absence would doubtless raise questions as to why you chose to avoid being here."

"I'll . . . I'll come, of course," Musgrove mumbled, unnerved. "I didn't realize this was such . . . such an important meeting."

"I'm sure you didn't. Mr. Wolfe will be pleased to hear you will be with us tomorrow night."

The next thing on my chore list was a call to—believe it or not—Franco Bacelli. Somewhere, Wolfe had located a telephone number for him, which I dialed, figuring I'd end up talking to some underling. But to my surprise, the prince of darkness himself answered.

"You gotta be kiddin' me!" he said when I extended the invitation. "You mean your fat boss really expects me to be there while he tries to pin the killing on this old Sicilian. Forget it."

"But when you were here before, I thought you claimed you are clean on the shooting."

"You're damned right I am, pal."

"Then what have you got to fear? I seem to remember you saying you never cover your face with a newspaper when photographers are around."

"That's right. I don't and never have. Who else is going to be at this shindig of Wolfe's?"

"No photographers, but a room full of interested parties. You'll just have to see for yourself."

"Any cops?"

"Very likely," I said. "Inspector Cramer has been known to drop by."

"Cramer!" he snorted. "I think it would be worth coming just to see the expression on that old flatfoot's face when I walk into the room. All right, what the devil, I'll be there."

"Remember, it will be like last time, we are letting only you in, and not any of your . . . colleagues."

"Okay, that's a deal. Are you gonna try to frisk me?" he asked, laughing.

"No, I don't think so. After all, you'll be outnumbered."

Another laugh. "Hey, even when I'm outnumbered, I'm not really outnumbered. How do you think I've survived this long?"

"We'll expect you at nine tomorrow," I said, hanging up and turning to Wolfe. "Well, they're all coming, every last one of them. It seems that nobody can resist a good show."

He put down his book, drew in air, and uttered a single word: "Hubris."

CHAPTER 28

Nero Wolfe loves to perform before an audience, and he would have a big one this June evening. He had taken it upon himself to invite Inspector Lionel T. Cramer and Sergeant Purley Stebbins, bringing the number of guests to twelve—or thirteen if you counted our "special mystery guest," a term I'm stealing from that brand-new television quiz show *What's My Line?*

While Wolfe was in the plant rooms that afternoon, I set up extra chairs in the office, two rows facing his desk plus, of course, the red leather chair. I restocked the cocktail cart along one wall with fresh ice and a variety of liquors and mixes.

I then went down the hall, almost to the kitchen, to check the curtained alcove that hides what we call "the peephole." In the alcove, one can look through a small hole in a painting of the Washington Monument hanging on an office wall and see and hear what goes on in the office. The hole is undetectable from inside the office. We have used this simple but effective device on numerous occasions, both to eavesdrop on conversations and to watch the reactions of those who think they are alone. Our mystery guest would be in the alcove tonight.

Next, I put in a call to Lon Cohen. "Got yourself any plans for this evening?" I asked.

"Nothing special, why? Am I invited to dinner again?"

"Don't be so greedy. You were just here, and our grocery budget is still recovering. Wolfe has invited all the principals in the Milbank case to the brownstone tonight, and we just may have some news for you later."

"In that case, I will be at my desk waiting for your call."

Invariably, when one of these events is scheduled, I find myself growing more nervous as the day drags on. Not so for Nero Wolfe. To see him at dinner, devouring lamb chops with walnuts or pork stewed in beer, you would never think he was preparing to unmask a murderer in less than two hours. His conversation at the table on such an evening might range from how the routes of the railroads affected the growth of America to various theories on why audiences invariably rise when the "Hallelujah" chorus from Handel's *Messiah* is performed.

At eight thirty, Saul Panzer arrived with our mystery guest, whom he ushered to the kitchen, where said guest would remain until all the others were in place. Saul then joined me in the greeting and seating duties. The first to arrive, Charles and Mona Fentress, warily stepped in, both looking like they would much rather be elsewhere. Elise

DuVal was right behind them. She kissed me on the cheek and glowered at Mona, who pointedly ignored her.

Then in quick succession came a snarling Jonah Keller, a nervous Keith Musgrove, a somber Ross Davies, a puzzled Todd Armstrong, and a gregarious Ray Corcoran, who pumped my hand and said he felt "privileged" to be invited.

As I stood on the stoop looking out into the twilight, a black Lincoln eased smoothly to the curb and Franco Bacelli stepped out, grinning up at me and doffing his black homburg.

"Bet you thought I wouldn't show, eh? Well, I'm here and I'm unarmed," he cackled, throwing open the jacket of his pinstriped silk suit to show me a silver lining and empty pockets. He bounded up to the door and winked as he entered the house. By my count, that left only the law enforcement pair, who always arrived late, and Howell Baxter, the open-spaces lover from CLEAN.

"I'm here, city boy, I'm here!" Baxter yelled as he jogged toward the brownstone, waving his arms. "I told you I don't get down to this town very often, and I always find myself all turned around when I do. On top of that, my train into Grand Central was behind schedule. Sorry to be late," he said as he came up the steps, panting. He wore an ill-fitting sport coat and a rumpled shirt, but he had put on a tie for the occasion, likely the only one he owned.

As I ushered Baxter in, I turned to see a spartan Ford sedan pull up behind Bacelli's Lincoln. Cramer and Stebbins climbed out, both of them wearing dark suits and frowns. "You're just in time," I told them. "Although we were not going to start without you."

Cramer lumbered in, not bothering to acknowledge my presence, and the square-faced Stebbins followed suit. Stebbins and I have cordially disliked each other for years, rarely exchanging more than a few words in all that time. We both are fine with the arrangement.

When I closed and locked the front door and went to the office, I found Saul had gotten everyone seated except Cramer and Stebbins, who stood with their backs against the wall, focusing their attention and animosity on a smirking Franco Bacelli, who seemed to be relishing the stares he was getting from everyone around him.

Elise DuVal sat in the red leather chair, befitting her position as client. The front row consisted of Franco Bacelli, Howell Baxter, Jonah Keller, Keith Musgrove, and Ross Davies. Parked in the second row were Ray Corcoran, Todd Armstrong, and Charles and Mona Fentress. "Where is Nero Wolfe?" Keller demanded. "Let's get this show going."

"He is on his way," I said, moving to Wolfe's desk and reaching under his center drawer to push the buzzer, which would bring him from the kitchen to make his entrance.

Thirty seconds later, he strode in, detoured around the desk, and rang for beer. "Thank you all for coming," he said as he looked around, dipping his chin slightly toward each person in turn. "Who are they?" Musgrove squeaked, turning and tilting his head toward the members of New York's Finest.

"Inspector Cramer of the Homicide Squad and his associate Sergeant Stebbins," Wolfe said as he sat. "They are present at my invitation and remain with my forbearance. Do you have any objection to their being present?"

Musgrove rolled his eyes and shook his head but said nothing more.

"What about him?" Charles Fentress growled, pointing a thumb in Bacelli's direction.

"What about him indeed, Mr. Fentress?" Wolfe countered. "Does his presence discommode you?"

"I . . . oh, what the heck, this is your show," the advertising executive said, waving a palm dismissively. "We're just a bunch of bystanders, wondering why in heaven's name we're here."

"I hope by the time we have concluded, all of you will have a better understanding of the reason we have gathered. But before we continue, would anyone like refreshments? As you can see, I am having beer. Mr. Goodwin and Mr. Panzer can serve you."

The enthusiasm surprised me. Both Fentresses asked for scotch, Elise had a gin and tonic, Bacelli called for a glass of water with ice, Keller ordered an old-fashioned, and Corcoran, Davies, and Baxter opted for beer. Musgrove and Armstrong took a pass. After the orders were filled—and efficiently, I might add—Saul left the office and Wolfe sat back, surveying the gathering once more.

"From the beginning of my investigation into the shooting of Senator Orson Milbank, I strove to determine a motive and found it difficult to ascertain one," he said. "I agree that—"

"What do you mean?" Cramer rumbled. "The man had alienated damned near everybody with his waffling on that parkway. And that includes Bacelli here." He spoke the mobster's name as if it were contagious.

"As I started to say before you interrupted me, sir, I agree that Mr. Milbank angered many people because of his various positions regarding the road," Wolfe said evenly. "But not since frontier times in this country have people killed one another over the proposed route of a road or a railway. And many of those who did the killing represented competing turnpikes or rail lines."

"So nice to hear that you are able to pontificate about American history, but just what are you getting at?" Charles Fentress asked in a belligerent tone before taking a sip of his scotch.

"Be patient, sir, as I explain."

"Yeah, whatever you do, for God's sake, don't interrupt him," Cramer put in. "You'll want to get home before dawn."

"I will not detain any of you longer than necessary," Wolfe pronounced, pouring beer into a pilsner glass from one of the two bottles Fritz had brought in. "Before I continue, I confess that I, too, initially accepted the idea that his attitudes about the Northern Parkway likely caused the senator's death. Never mind that during my investigation, several people, including Mr. Goodwin, questioned whether a fight over a road was sufficient stimulus to provoke someone to murder. I was deaf to their comments until I finally determined to my satisfaction that the road had nothing whatever to do with Senator Milbank's violent death."

"Hear, hear!" Bacelli cut in, clapping his hands. "Thank the good Lord somebody in this room has some sense," he added, turning to glare at Cramer.

It was Wolfe's turn to glare—at Bacelli. "You, like the police, are here at my sufferance, sir. Another outburst, and I will ask Mr. Goodwin to remove you from the premises. He has had practice doing so on previous occasions in this room, and he is most efficient at the task." The color rose in Bacelli's cheeks, and he covered any embarrassment by taking a gulp of his water.

"Now if I may continue," Wolfe said, "once I

came to my senses and felt the issue over the parkway was not the reason for Mr. Milbank's death, I turned to his private life in search of a motive. It was made known to me that the senator and Mrs. Fentress had become something of an item, at least in the minds of newspaper columnists and gossip mongers."

"I like the way you phrased that," Charles Fentress said sourly, raising his glass in a mock salute as his wife the candidate hunkered down in her chair, probably wishing she could become invisible.

Wolfe ignored the interruption. "I considered this real or imagined relationship as a possible motive for taking a man's life but dismissed it as tabloid fodder. Was that a wise decision on my part?" Wolfe asked, flipping a palm. "I do not believe it was, particularly now." He readjusted his bulk and drank more beer.

"So then, just who was responsible for killing Orson?" Keller demanded, leaning forward and jabbing a finger in Wolfe's direction like a prosecuting attorney zeroing in on a witness.

"Bear with me. Let us return to that fateful afternoon at the Polo Grounds. As we now know, a marksman lurked, presumably unnoticed, in the shadows of the stadium's roofed and empty upper deck in left field, some two hundred eighty feet from where Mr. Milbank and his party were seated. The marksman, a decorated war veteran named Richard Thompson, was found dead in his Queens home just over a week ago, a suicide."

"Who was this Thompson and how do you know this?" Cramer demanded.

"I will get to that, sir, as well as to how Mr. Thompson happened to be the shooter."

"How did Thompson know Orson?" Elise DuVal asked.

"He did not know him and had almost surely never met him," Wolfe said.

"So it was a hit," Bacelli put in, slapping a palm on his knee. "The guy was a hired gun, plain and simple."

"You of all people would know all about that," Sergeant Stebbins said, reaching under his suit jacket in the vicinity of his shoulder holster.

"If many of you insist on interrupting, that is all right with me," Wolfe said. "Clearly, I am not going anywhere."

"Okay, okay, get on with it," Cramer said. "I for one would like to see my bed before the sun rises."

"Thank you. The shooter—or alleged shooter if you prefer, Inspector—was a marine known for and cited for his accuracy with a rifle. He was a sniper who had won medals for his bravery on Okinawa. A year ago, he was one of many local veterans who got honored at a dinner at the Waldorf Astoria organized by the *Gazette*. I salute Mr. Goodwin's resourcefulness in determining that several of you in this room were at that dinner."

"Not me!" Bacelli snapped.

"No, sir, not you. But among those in attendance were Mr. and Mrs. Fentress and Messrs. Keller and Corcoran."

"Yes, we both were there," Mona said, "but so were hundreds of others. By the way, Charles and I were not together at that event. His advertising agency hosted a table, and I sat at Orson's table. He was a big supporter of the banquet and distributed small flags to all of the veterans."

"Sure, I was there, too," Keller put in, "hosting a table of veterans from Westchester and Putnam Counties, and I'm proud of it. Great young men, every one of them, the hope of our country's future. It was a privilege to be with them."

"And I also was present," Corcoran added. "I'm active with a VFW post up north, as Mr. Goodwin knows, and I had a table full of medal winners. I agree with Jonah that these young men are the backbone of our nation."

"All right, if we are all through congratulating ourselves and one another for honoring our heroes, let's move on," Cramer said, turning to Wolfe. "As Mrs. Fentress points out, there were hundreds in that ballroom. Is it so surprising that some of these people were among them?"

"Not in and of itself," Wolfe conceded. "Still, it is worth asking these four if any one of them happened to sit at the same table with Richard Thompson." He looked at the quartet and they all shook their heads. "Was he from Westchester or Putnam?" Keller asked.

"No, sir," Wolfe said. "I already have stated his home was in Queens."

"So there you are," Keller snapped. "As I just said, all the veterans at my table were from up north. Now let's get on with this, as the inspector says. I can't see that we're making any progress."

"Very well," Wolfe said. "Because of activities I was involved in long ago almost halfway around the world, I have learned something of the modus operandi of snipers, and—"

"So now we're about to get a lesson in gunnery?" Corcoran said, apparently to show he could be just as feisty as Keller.

"Only insofar as it helps to explain the events of that afternoon," Wolfe replied. "My appearance belies this, but at one time in my youth, I was involved in what historians often euphemis-tically term a revolutionary movement, one that involved guerrilla warfare. I became a good shot with a rifle—indeed, a very good shot. One of the things I learned quickly—and a fact many of you surely also know—is that marks-men are taught to aim at the upper trunk of the victim rather than the head, the trunk being the far broader target."

"But Orson was shot . . . in the head," Elise

DuVal said in a voice barely above a whisper.

Wolfe nodded. "Precisely, and in the left temple, not straight on, indicating that he was not facing the playing field when he was shot." He turned to Ross Davies. "I have been informed that Mrs. Fentress was on the senator's right, and you were on her right. Is that correct?"

"Yes, I've been asked that several times before, including by him," Davies said, nodding toward Cramer. "And by you as well, Mr. Wolfe."

"Humor me, please, sir. Describe to all of us what happened at the moment Senator Milbank was shot."

Davies pulled in air and looked around the room for sympathy. Seeing none, he turned to Wolfe. "Where should I start?"

"At the time the home run was hit, in—when was it?—the fourth inning."

"Yes, the fourth. Reed Mason really nailed the ball, and we all stood to watch it go over the fence. Mona suddenly toppled over against me— we later learned that the heel of her right shoe had snapped off."

"That's exactly what happened," Mona said, "and I just plain lost my balance."

"I've heard a lot about that famous so-called broken heel," Elise cut in, sneering. "But did anyone ever actually see it?"

"Oh, I did," Davies said. "It had snapped just like that, a clean break. It was at that moment that we realized Orson had been shot. Oh my God, it was awful."

"Is it really necessary to make people relive all this?" Keller demanded, starting to rise.

"Sit down!" Cramer barked. Keller sat.

"Now I believe you were on the senator's left, Mr. Armstrong."

The young man nodded. "Yes, and when he got shot, he lurched to the right, away from me."

"Or did he lurch to the right *before* he was shot?"

"I . . . I really don't know. Everything happened so fast. Even now, I have trouble reconstructing what happened."

"Just what are you getting at, Mr. Wolfe?" Corcoran asked.

"I am taking the position that the senator reflexively leaned over Mrs. Fentress's seat to try to catch her as she fell away from him."

"We have been over all of this before," Cramer interjected. "I don't see the point of it."

"The point, sir, is that Mr. Milbank was not the target of the gunshot."

CHAPTER 29

If the intention of that comment had been to send the group into frenzy, it succeeded in spades. Although Wolfe remained expressionless, I knew he was enjoying the stir he had created, and he was in no hurry to see it end. Not so the case with Inspector Cramer.

"All right, all right!" the grizzled cop bellowed over the cacophony. "I realize that like the rest of you, I am an invited guest in this house. But I also am an officer of the law with certain fairly well-defined responsibilities, one of which is to identify and arrest—if possible—suspected murderers. Since this is your show, Wolfe, go on. And what comes had damned well better be good enough to have brought us all here."

"Before you go any farther with whatever explanation you've got," a suddenly emboldened Musgrove said, "I have to ask why the shooter waited until the fourth inning. We all had been in our seats since the start of the game, which was at least forty-five or fifty minutes earlier."

"He was biding his time in the upper deck, waiting for people to stand so he would have a better target," Wolfe said.

"But what if nobody hit a home run or did anything else exciting? Then the crowd would never stand up at all," the little pollster persisted.

"Even if nothing had happened in the game to bring the crowd to its feet, the shooter would have eventually gotten his chance during the seventh-inning stretch," I put in. "Everybody stands then."

"I would like to hear Mr. Wolfe talk more about who he thinks was the real target," Elise said.

"Thank you, madam," he said. "How tall was your husband?"

"That's a strange question, but . . . well, he was six foot three."

"And how tall are you, Mrs. Fentress, when wearing your high-heeled shoes?" Wolfe asked.

"About five eight, why?"

"As unpleasant as the memories are, let us return once more to that afternoon at the Polo Grounds. The shooter, who had gotten into the ball park undetected and was ensconced well back in the shadows of the upper reaches, was prepared to wait until such time as the crowd rose, including the Milbank party. His job was made all the easier given that they were in the front row, with nothing between them and the barrel of his .30 caliber rifle. When the home run was hit and everyone leaped to their feet, he took aim and fired, but in that millisecond, his target had moved."

"Me?" gasped Mona, jerking upright, her normally lovely face contorted in disbelief.

"You, madam," Wolfe pronounced. "You were

indeed the target, but when you fell sideways after your heel had snapped, Senator Milbank reached across to catch you, and as he bent over, his head was precisely where your chest had been only an instant before. He was facing you, not the field, and the bullet entered his left temple."

"This is ridiculous speculation!" Charles Fentress bayed. "Of course, Milbank was the target."

"Don't interrupt," Cramer said. "Let him go on."

"The shooter was hired to kill Mrs. Fentress by someone in this room," Wolfe said, looking at the picture of the Washington Monument and rubbing the right side of his nose with his index finger. A signal.

Seconds later, the door to the hall opened and Saul Panzer stepped in, followed by a stone-faced Marguerite Hackman.

"What is all this about?" Cramer demanded, scowling at Panzer and Mrs. Hackman.

"Your forbearance please," Wolfe said, holding up a hand. "Madam, thank you for coming. Did you hear a familiar voice?"

She nodded and pointed to Charles Fentress. "That's the one."

"What are you talking about?" Fentress shouted, getting to his feet. Sergeant Stebbins quickly moved behind him, laying a hand on his shoulder and pushing him back into his chair.

"This woman, Marguerite Hackman, is the sister of Richard Thompson, who for the last year or so lived in her house in the Flushing neighborhood of Queens," Wolfe said. "Thompson had received several telephone calls and a visit from a man I believe hired him to shoot Mona Fentress. Mrs. Hackman answered these calls on several occasions, and she has been observing—and hearing—our conversation from a vantage just outside this room."

"This is ridiculous!" Fentress ranted. "Trying to blame someone based on a voice. Hellfire, there have to be hundreds, maybe thousands, of men in the area who sound like me."

"That is him," Mrs. Hackman insisted. "I know it."

A shaken Mona Fentress turned to Marguerite Hackman. "I have a question for you," she said in a halting voice. "Did your brother stutter?"

"Yes, yes, he did, badly, but that happened only after he came back from the Pacific. The war had made him a different person, and not in a good way."

"You bastard!" Mona screamed, standing and slapping her husband across the face as he put up an arm to protect himself. "You miserable bastard!" She slapped him again and stopped only when Sergeant Stebbins wrapped his arms around her and pulled her away.

She ran a hand through disheveled hair and looked down at the cowering advertising executive. "Three different times, a man with a stutter

277

called at home to talk to you when you were away. He wouldn't leave his name, but if you remember, I told you about it and even mentioned the stutter. You claimed he was an artist your agency had hired. Hah!"

The fire had gone out of Charles Fentress, who sat rubbing his red cheek and shaking his head. "Why?" his wife said to him in tears. "Why?"

"Inspector, you will, I am sure, fill in the details, but let me suggest this scenario," Wolfe said. "Mr. Fentress had wanted to marry another woman, Caroline Jackson Willis. This meant getting rid of his current wife."

"For God's sake, Charles, I would have divorced you in a minute!" Mona screamed. "I . . . I . . ."

Wolfe waited several beats before continuing. "There is more to this. Mr. Fentress also wanted to inflict the ultimate punishment upon his wife for her suspected affair with Senator Milbank, never mind that he was conducting a liaison of his own. He could not stand the idea that he was being cuckolded, and his anger manifested itself in public outbursts against Mr. Milbank, purportedly because the senator was working Mona Fentress too hard."

Wolfe paused to drink beer, then went on. "Somehow, perhaps at that Waldorf Astoria dinner, Mr. Fentress met Richard Thompson, a decorated sharpshooter whose life since the war had been in a downward spiral. It is likely that

Charles Fentress saw in this deeply troubled young man someone whom he could use in the future, and someone who was in need of money.

"The opportunity to put the sharpshooter's skill to use came when Mr. Fentress learned of the visit to the baseball game by Senator Milbank and his staff. He called Mr. Thompson and even visited him once at his home in Queens. It may have taken some persuasion on Charles Fentress's part, probably in the form of promises of ever-increasing amounts of money, but eventually, Mr. Thompson was worn down and agreed to the assignment. It was at this time that the former marine confided to his sister that 'something big' was in his future."

Marguerite Hackman, still standing rigidly next to Saul Panzer, nodded, expressionless.

"How Mr. Thompson was able to enter the Polo Grounds so easily was not a problem, given that he had once been employed at that stadium, albeit briefly, in a custodial capacity," Wolfe said. "It turns out that he had kept a key during his brief time working for the Giants, a key that would grant him entry into the outfield grandstands. This explains how he got into the stadium so easily.

"In his fragile emotional state, Mr. Thompson must have been extremely nervous as he crouched, well out of sight in the shadows of the ball park's upper deck," Wolfe continued. "When the time finally came to shoot, he was surely horrified when he hit the wrong person. He undoubtedly fled from the stadium quickly, not bothering to relock the gate he had opened."

"He should have been horrified that he was even in that position to begin with," Davies said.

Wolfe nodded. "True, but bear in mind that this was a man who, with little regard for his own safety, had put his life on the line for his country during one of the most violent and deadly campaigns of the last war, Okinawa, and that he was so badly scarred by the experience he could no longer be considered rational by any reasonable standard."

"Of course, you are right," Davies said. "A lot of men who have come back from the war without physical wounds have been permanently damaged nonetheless. I saw it myself both during combat and back at home."

"After the killing, Charles Fentress was angry at Richard Thompson but was relieved in the sense that everyone would think the senator had been the target," Wolfe continued. "In fact, Mr. Fentress probably felt that if his wife had indeed been the victim as intended, the police and the public would assume the shot had been intended for Mr. Milbank and went awry. He felt he could not lose either way."

Fentress sat, arms folded and face down. Sergeant Stebbins had not moved from his side.

"So Richard Thompson was so distraught at

what had happened that he killed himself?" Ray Corcoran asked.

"He was driven to it by that man!" Marguerite Hackman said, glaring at Fentress. "He called the evening Dick shot himself, the same day as the shooting at the baseball game, June 14. I answered the phone and when I told Dick it was for him, he made me leave the room. I remember that he seemed hysterical even before he picked up the receiver. How I wish I had just hung up on you," she spat at Fentress.

Wolfe continued. "Inspector, I believe Mrs. Hackman to be correct in her assertion that Richard Thompson was encouraged to end his life. After all, he now was a murderer, with virtually no hope of avoiding either permanent imprisonment or death. Let us assume Mr. Fentress presented him with that grim prospect during that telephone conversation, as was probably the case. Faced with that kind of future, it is not at all difficult to imagine the young man using his service pistol to ensure he would never go to trial."

"Say what you want to, this was not truly a suicide, it was murder!" the dead marine's sister insisted.

"How did you know about the Thompson suicide?" Cramer asked.

"From a newspaper death notice," Wolfe replied. "It seemed more than a coincidence that a veteran noted for his proficiency with a rifle should kill himself on the same night as the shooting at the baseball game. That the police in Queens did not pick up on this is hardly surprising, especially given that far too many servicemen continue to commit suicide, even almost a half decade after the war's end."

"What about the weapon?" Cramer asked.

"Mrs. Hackman has what almost surely is the murder weapon, a M1 Garand rifle that belonged to her brother, and I'm sure she will give it to you," Wolfe said, looking at the woman. She nodded.

"Not that we could prove anything by having it," Cramer said. "It's been days now since it was used. Besides, that bullet could have been fired by almost any .30 caliber weapon. But still, we want it."

"It is yours, to do with as you will," Marguerite Hackman said. "I do not want to see it ever again. And I also do not want to see that man ever again," she added, indicating Charles Fentress.

"Assuming for a moment that the shot *had* killed Mrs. Fentress, what was her husband's plan for keeping Thompson quiet?" Cramer asked.

"Perhaps you will learn that, Inspector," Wolfe said. "My surmise is that Charles Fentress would have used the same tactics to get Mr. Thompson to end his life as he did after Senator Milbank's death."

"I feel like I'm in some sort of damned kangaroo

court," Charles Fentress said, sitting up straight and suddenly reverting to his combative stance. "Nothing that was said here tonight about my presumed actions can be proven. Everything is totally surmise, a setup, probably engineered by my dear wife," he said, turning to scowl at Mona. "I want a lawyer."

"Oh, you will get a lawyer," Cramer said. "Purley, put the cuffs on him and let's go."

As Charles Fentress was led away, his wife stood and watched his back, her face a mixture of sadness and loathing. Although I was not overly fond of Mona Fentress, I could not help but feel sympathy for the woman.

"Well, this has been quite the show," Bacelli said to Wolfe as he rose and rubbed his palms together. "Very entertaining. I told you before that I had nothing to do with the senator's death."

"First, I am pleased to hear that you were entertained tonight, although I assure you that such was not my intent. Second, I never seriously considered you to be a suspect, but I felt this evening might give you some idea of what is in store for you in a far different setting."

"So now you're a comedian, huh?" Bacelli snarled. "We'll see who gets the last laugh." He turned on his heel and marched out.

The others, some of them visibly amused at the byplay between Wolfe and the Mob boss, began to file out. Marguerite Hackman hung back and waited until all of them except Elise DuVal had gone down the hall, where Saul Panzer would usher them out.

"Mr. Wolfe, thank you very much both for what you did tonight and what you said about Dick. These last few years were terrible for him," Mrs. Hackman said.

"I can only imagine what you have gone through, madam," he said. "As a nation, we sadly lack in giving our service personnel the kind of postwar care they richly merit."

"Dick was a fine marine."

"I do not doubt that for a moment. In wartime, we cannot say enough about the bravery and valor of our fighting forces. But once the armistice comes, they become invisible to the public, never mind that many of them have been permanently damaged, both physically and psychologically."

She nodded and gave Wolfe a thin smile that had no happiness behind it, then left the office. I walked her down the hall to the door, and as I opened it, she put a hand on my arm. "Even during your first trip to my house, when I realized you were not what you claimed to be, I could tell you were a good man. That is why I let you come back, and I am glad that I did. Thank you for everything you have done." She turned and went down the steps to the street, her destination the empty house in Flushing.

Back in the office, Elise DuVal, still in the red

leather chair, was jawing with Wolfe. "Well, you did it," she said. "I never would have guessed it was Charles Fentress. Did you know from the beginning?"

"No, although of all those who were involved in this sad business, he seemed to be the most morally bankrupt—other than Franco Bacelli, of course."

"And as you told Bacelli, you really never seriously considered him a suspect?"

"I did not, even when I still believed Senator Milbank to be the intended victim. Mr. Bacelli is currently far too occupied with fighting other battles, courtroom battles he is almost sure to lose."

"Well, you have both my thanks and a well-deserved fee," she said standing. "Goodnight."

I walked her to the door. "Remember," she said, "you are going to buy me dinner."

"Yes, and I'm sure you just can't wait to tell Lily Rowan about that, can you?"

"Why, Archie, why ever would I want to do that?"

"Because you're you," I said, smiling. "But at the risk of puncturing your balloon, I already told her."

"You're a killjoy, Archie Goodwin. That's what you are."

"Maybe, but as I told you before, I can dance up a storm. If you don't believe me, just ask Lily."

CHAPTER 30

With everyone gone from the brownstone, I called Lon Cohen, who picked up before the first ring had stopped. I gave him a rundown on the events of the evening, and after I had unloaded, he gave me a quick thank-you and set off to put the news-gathering machinery of America's fifth-largest newspaper in motion. The man would have his scoop, as promised by Nero Wolfe.

After a marathon grilling by the police, Charles Fentress spilled the works. It turned out that he had met Richard Thompson when they sat at the same table at that Waldorf Astoria banquet. Fentress learned in their conversation about Thompson's having worked briefly at both the Polo Grounds and Yankee Stadium, and the ex-GI had bragged that he still had keys to both stadiums, although he had never made use of either one. At the time, that seemingly meaningless fact meant nothing to Fentress, but he filed it away and it later became significant to him.

Fentress's confession saved the state the cost of a trial, and his high-powered Manhattan lawyer helped him escape the electric chair, although he did get life in prison and now resides in a cell at Sing Sing prison up on the Hudson north of the city, where he has plenty of time to reflect upon his sins.

Franco Bacelli also got himself one of the best and most successful defense lawyers in all of New York, but Bacelli and his slick mouthpiece had the misfortune of going up against our ambitious new federal prosecutor, who was out to make a name for himself. He certainly did during that highly publicized case, nailing the Mob boss on a fistful of charges. Bacelli's lawyer appealed the decision without success, with the result that the former Mob kingpin now resides at the federal penitentiary in Atlanta, at least fortunate that he didn't get sent to the even worse fate of Alcatraz, that island fortress in San Francisco Bay that houses the worst of the worst in the criminal world.

As for Mona Fentress, she was handily beaten in her campaign for Milbank's senate seat. According to Lon Cohen, the *Gazette*'s political editor felt she had been undone by all the publicity surrounding Milbank's death, along with her rumored affair with him and also her husband's murder conviction. But she was unbowed in the face of her defeat, saying that she would fight on.

"Orson Milbank's legacy is just too big, too important, to be cast aside like yesterday's newspaper," she said in her impassioned concession speech. "I will be back to carry the

Milbank banner forward. I promise that you have not heard the last of Mona Fentress."

Regarding the Northern Parkway, at present it survives only on the drawing boards of the state's civil engineering department. Increased cost estimates and continuing disputes over its precise route have led to a stalemate in the New York legislature. Both Jonah Keller and Ray Corcoran often get quoted in the newspapers decrying the inaction of the politicians and stressing the importance of the highway to those counties that lie just north of the city.

Just last week, the *New York Times* ran a three-column photograph of a group of perky coeds from Vassar marching in front of the state capitol in Albany. They carried signs on sticks reading PARKS NOT ROADS! and MONEY FOR SCHOOLS YES, FOR HIGHWAYS NO. In the background, I spotted Howell Baxter, lugging a sign and grinning like the victor in a war.

For the record, I did have that dinner with Elise DuVal, and in a private room upstairs at Rusterman's, no less. Between courses, she confided that Lily Rowan had told her I was harmless.

"You know," I said, "a comment like that plays havoc with the image I'm trying to develop as a devil-may-care bon vivant, boulevardier, and man about town."

"I promise, Archie, that I won't tell anyone

else," she said, fluttering her eyelashes. "Besides, even if you weren't harmless, it wouldn't matter. I have developed a crush on Nero Wolfe."

"Too bad, he's already taken. He has concubines."

Her mouth dropped open. "Are you serious?"

"Dead serious. There are ten thousand in all. Maybe Lily has told you about them. They are the orchids in the plant rooms up on the roof of the brownstone, in three temperature-controlled rooms. You will have to see them someday to fully appreciate what you are up against, and I would be happy to arrange a visit. You are a lovely and desirable woman, but give this up before you embarrass yourself. As beautiful as you are, you do not stand the proverbial snowball's chance in hell against those exotic beauties."

AUTHOR NOTES

This story is set at the approximate midpoint of the twentieth century, roughly a half decade after the end of World War II, near the outset of the Korean War, and a handful of years before the New York Giants and Brooklyn Dodgers baseball teams deserted their longtime hometown for San Francisco and Los Angeles respectively.

Northern Manhattan's Polo Grounds, site of the narrative's murder, had been home to the baseball Giants from 1911 until they migrated to California in 1957. The New York Yankees also were tenants of the ball park from 1913 until 1922; they moved across the Harlem River into the newly completed Yankee Stadium in the Bronx in 1923. The New York Mets played their first two seasons in the Polo Grounds, 1962–1963, before moving to the new Shea Stadium in the Flushing Meadows–Corona Park neighborhood of Queens in 1964.

The Polo Grounds also hosted several professional football teams: the New York Giants of the National Football League from 1925 to 1955 and the NFL's New York Bulldogs in 1949. The New York Titans (later Jets) of the American Football League played in the Polo Grounds from 1960 to 1963.

The Polo Grounds often was referred to by

journalists and fans as "Coogan's Bluff" because that was the name of a promontory, or cliff, that overlooked the ball park and provided nonpaying spectators a view of the action far below on the field.

The most famous moment in the venerable stadium's history came on October 3, 1951, when Bobby Thomson of the baseball Giants hit a three-run homer ("the shot heard round the world") with two outs in the bottom of the ninth inning against the Brooklyn Dodgers to give the Giants a 5–4 victory and the National League pennant in the third and final game of a playoff series to determine the championship. The teams had finished in a first-place tie at the end of the regular season. The Thomson home run was hit to approximately the same spot in the close-in left-field stands as the home run in this story that immediately preceded the murder of New York State Senator Orson Milbank.

Nero Wolfe–creator Rex Stout, who was an avid baseball fan, placed one of his Wolfe tales at the Polo Grounds. The novella "This Won't Kill You," from the trilogy *Three Men Out* (1954), is set against the backdrop of a fictional World Series between the New York Giants and Boston Red Sox and involves a murder at the ball park. Wolfe is obligated to attend the seventh and deciding game of the series because a house guest and friend, famed Paris restaurateur Pierre

Mondor, has asked to see a baseball game. Archie Goodwin reports that Wolfe must suffer through sitting on the front edge of a seat at the ball park because his girth will not fit between the armrests. Uncom-fortable or not, he overcomes that adversity to solve the crime—the killing of one of the Giants' players.

According to his biographer, the late John McAleer, Rex Stout was "an ardent Giants fan," and both his daughters add that he disliked the New York Yankees. McAleer wrote that when the Giants and Dodgers moved to California, Stout switched his allegiance to the new Mets team.

The Polo Grounds was demolished in April 1964, and the site is now occupied by the Polo Grounds Towers, a housing complex comprising four high-rise buildings.

All of the characters and events in this story are fictional, and no person is modeled on a specific individual. The Northern Parkway also is fictional and should not be confused with the Adirondack Northway (Interstate 87), which began construc-tion in the 1950s and which runs more than 330 miles north from New York City to the Canadian border.

With the exception of Lon Cohen's *Gazette*, a fictional newspaper that plays a role in many Nero Wolfe stories, all of the other newspapers mentioned either exist or did exist at the time of this novel's setting.

As with all of my previous Nero Wolfe stories, my heartfelt thanks go to Barbara Stout and Rebecca Stout Bradbury for their support and encouragement. My thanks also go to my agent, Erik Simon of the Martha Kaplan Agency, for his tireless efforts and wise council; to Otto Penzler and Rob Hart of MysteriousPress.com for their guidance; and to the great team at Open Road Integrated Media for their work on the editing, production, and promotion of the book. A special note of gratitude to longtime friend and encourager Max Allan Collins, a son of Iowa and a filmmaker and mystery writer extraordinaire, who had made invaluable suggestions and to whom this book is warmly and deservedly dedicated.

A tip of the hat to lifelong friend and ace competitive marksman Ray Rausch, who reminded me of the significance to American troops during World War II of the iconic M1 Garand rifle, which I myself toted, cleaned, and slept with during army basic training. And most of all, thanks and love to my wife, Janet, who for a half century has been a constant source of encouragement and inspiration, even in my grouchiest moods, of which there have been more than a few.

As has been the case with my earlier Nero Wolfe stories, I found several books to be particularly helpful as references:

Nero Wolfe of West Thirty-Fifth Street: The Life and Times of America's Largest Private Detective by William S. Baring-Gould (Viking Press, 1969); *The Brownstone House of Nero Wolfe* by Ken Darby (Little, Brown & Co., 1983); *The Nero Wolfe Cookbook* by Rex Stout and the Editors of Viking Press (Viking Press, 1973); and the excellent biography *Rex Stout* by the afore-mentioned John J. McAleer (Little, Brown & Co., 1977), which deservedly won a Mystery Writers of America Edgar Award for the best critical/ autobiographical work in 1978.

Center Point Large Print
600 Brooks Road / PO Box 1
Thorndike ME 04986-0001 USA

(207) 568-3717

US & Canada:
1 800 929-9108
www.centerpointlargeprint.com